HENRY JAMES
THE REVERBERATOR

With an Introductory Note by
Simon Nowell-Smith

Grove Press, Inc.
New York

OTHER WORKS BY HENRY JAMES

PUBLISHED BY GROVE PRESS

Italian Hours

A London Life

The Sacred Fount

First Black Cat Edition 1979
First Printing 1979
ISBN: 0-394-17079-2
Grove Press ISBN: 0-8021-4241-9
Library of Congress Catalog Card Number: 57-6534

*The Library of Congress Cataloged the First Printing
of This Title as Follows:*
James, Henry, 1843–1916.

   The reverberator. With an introductory note by
Simon Nowell-Smith. New York, Grove Press [1957]

   x, 201 p.   22 cm.
"First printed...as a serial in Macmillan's magazine,
February–July 1888."
   I. Title
PZ3.J234Rev5   57-6534
Library of Congress   [2]

Manufactured in the United States of America

Distributed by Random House, Inc., New York

GROVE PRESS, INC., 196 West Houston Street,
New York, N.Y. 10014

INTRODUCTORY NOTE

I

THE New Journalism that invaded Europe from America in the eighteen-seventies was almost an inevitable subject for a novel by Henry James. In *The Portrait of a Lady*, written in 1880, Henrietta Stackpole hopes that her letters to the *New York Interviewer* about the way of life of the English nobility will be copied all over the West and make her the queen of American journalism. Planning another novel two or three years later James saw that no tally of contemporary Bostonians would be complete without 'a type of newspaper man, the man whose ideal is the energetic reporter. I should like to *bafouer* the vulgarity and hideousness of this, the impudent invasion of privacy, the extinction of all conception of privacy, etc.' The result was Matthias Pardon, who held that everything and everyone was everyone's business and of whom it was said that his indelicacy was his profession. But it is Henrietta herself, not any effects of her journalism, that contributes liveliness to *The Portrait of a Lady* (James later confessed that he had only introduced her, as a *ficelle du théâtre*, for liveliness' sake); and the impudences of Matthias Pardon belong rather to the lights and shades of local colour in *The Bostonians* than to the drama enacted by the principal characters. It is as though James was not yet ready to give his whole mind, or a whole novel, to the New Journalism; as though any real Stack-poles or Pardons he had so far known, or known of, had not touched him closely; as though a spark were needed to fire his imagination.

Before long two sparks were struck. In the winter after *The Bostonians* was published two examples of journalistic impudence came directly under his notice. Julian Hawthorne misreported in the press a confidential conversation with James Russell Lowell (recently American minister in London and destined to sit for a sympathetic portrait as the ambassador in James's *The Sense of the Past*); and an American girl who had been taken to the bosoms of the best families in Venice—where James stayed in two of the best houses in the course of the winter—wrote a chatty intimate account of that select and shockable society for a New York newspaper. James let several months pass before alluding to these events in his working notebook. When he did so he was still indignant, as a friend, over the 'beastly and blackguardly betrayal' of Lowell: but the other incident he had come to see with the detachment of a novelist in face of a *donnée*, so that the degree of flutter in the Venetian dovecote appealed as pregnantly to his ironic sense as did the injured innocence with which Miss McC— found her indiscretion regarded, by her victims, as an outrage.

Such were the germs of *The Reverberator*, and they were no more than merest germs. It would be as idle to identify Francie Dosson of Boston and 'Parus' with the obscure Miss McC— of New York and Venice, or the egregious George M. Flack of the *Reverberator* society-newspaper with the adequately documented Julian Hawthorne, as it would be to atomise old Mr Probert in the hope of isolating characteristics of Edward Lee Childe, Daniel Curtis (of Venice) and Henry James himself—the three men whom James thought of rolling into one to fill the part. George Flack's legitimate ancestor is Matthias Pardon, while Francie inherited her innocence and candour, and the defects of those qualities, from Daisy Miller.

The transmutation of two squalid little journalistic discourtesies of real life into the gem of comedy that is *The Reverberator* was achieved in two stages. The first is to be watched in the *Notebooks* entry for November 17th, 1887, where James, thinking aloud, plans a social international satire with a cynical climax; and the second may be deduced by comparing that half-formed plan with the published novel, a novel as romantic in its dénouement and as witty in its execution as anything he wrote. In his preface to the New York edition of 1908 James called his novel a *jeu d'esprit*.

II

The Reverberator was first printed (A) as a serial in *Macmillan's Magazine*, February-July 1888. Before the serial was completed Macmillans published, in May, a book edition in two volumes (B): the text of this shows some slight revision. Twenty years later, in 1908, the story was revised throughout for the definitive New York edition (C).

The text now reprinted is B, with obvious misprints corrected. On page 78 the reading of B, 'I shall never take to marry a Frenchwoman,' has been presumed to be wrong, as the reading of A ('like' for 'take') is confirmed by the expanded version of C, 'I shall never like to marry—when it comes to that—a Frenchwoman.' Most, though not all, of the revisions of 1908 involve expansion. They are in effect underlinings of passages that James seems to have come to suppose not lucid enough, or not emphatic enough. Often the expansion of a phrase, or even the interpolation of a whole sentence, is felicitous. Mr Probert, we are told on page 94, 'could bear French noise but he could not bear American. As for English, he maintained that there was none' (B). To this is added, in C, 'England was a country with the straw down in all the thoroughfares of talk.' Were all the revisions of this order, or were they merely such small touches of portraiture as making Delia Dosson address her parent as 'poppa' instead of 'father', there might be a case for preferring the final text. But in the twenty years between 1888 and 1908 James's 'manner' underwent a fundamental change. Whether it was a change for the better or the worse is a matter of opinion. It is a matter of opinion whether there was a gain or a loss of lucidity in altering 'the slightly surprised observer whom we have supposed to be present' (page 13) to 'the man of wonderments and measurements we have smuggled into the scene'; or in substituting for the statement that Gaston Probert 'had no jealousy of the insight which enabled [Waterlow] to reconstitute the girl on canvas with that perfection' (page 68) the statement that Gaston 'had no jealousy of the act of appropriation that rendered possible in its turn such an act of handing over, of which the canvas constituted the field'. It is matter of opinion whether in the following example—from the description of Delia on page 11—the gain in the subtle use of imagery, which is great, outweighs the loss, also great, of immediacy:

It was a plain, blank face, not only without movement, but with a suggestion of obstinacy in its repose; and yet, with its limitations, it was neither stupid nor displeasing. It had an air of intelligent calm—a considering, pondering look that was superior, somehow, to diffidence, or anxiety; moreover, the girl had a clear skin and a gentle, dim smile. (1888)

It was a plain clean round pattern face, marked for recognition among so many only perhaps by a small figure, the sprig on a china plate, that might have denoted deep obstinacy; and yet, with its settled smoothness, it was neither stupid nor hard. It was as calm as a room kept dusted and aired for candid earnest occasions, the meeting of unanimous committees and the discussion of flourishing businesses. (1908)

(Part of our loss in the later and longer version, be it

noted, is that we are told nothing either of Delia's complexion or of her smile.) It is matter of opinion also whether there is gain or loss of immediacy, or of euphony, in the numberless changes in recorded conversations, such as from 'Mr Dosson remarked, smiling' to 'Mr Dosson jocosely interjected', from 'commented Mme de Cliché' to 'shrilled implacably Mme de Cliché', from 'Francie demanded' to 'Francie beautifully gaped'. But it is matter of fact, not of opinion, that these and other remodelled phrases were the work of an older man than the author, in 1888, of *The Reverberator*, a man whose tortuosity of expression, alike in writing and in speech, had in the interval become legendary. That James's 'third manner' may be an essential part of the brilliance of later novels more brilliant perhaps in their way than *The Reverberator* is beside the point: the manner remains, for *The Reverberator*, an anachronism. And if the revisions of this novel of the late 'eighties are less drastic than those of the novels and stories of the 'seventies—*Roderick Hudson* and *The American*, *Daisy Miller* and *The Four Meetings*—they are still sufficient to alter the character of a narrative that depends, for its success as a *jeu d'esprit*, upon freshness of vision and lightness of touch.

SIMON NOWELL-SMITH

THE REVERBERATOR

I

'I GUESS my daughter's in here,' the old man said, leading the way into the little *salon de lecture*. He was not of the most advanced age, but that is the way George Flack considered him, and indeed he looked older than he was. George Flack had found him sitting in the court of the hotel (he sat a great deal in the court of the hotel), and had gone up to him with characteristic directness and asked him for Miss Francina. Poor Mr Dosson had with the greatest docility disposed himself to wait upon the young man: he had as a matter of course got up and made his way across the court, to announce to the personage in question that she had a visitor. He looked submissive, almost servile, as he preceded the visitor, thrusting his head forward in his quest; but it was not in Mr Flack's line to notice that sort of thing. He accepted the old gentleman's good offices as he would have accepted those of a waiter, murmuring no protest for the sake of making it appear that he had come to see him as well. An observer of these two persons would have assured himself that the degree to which Mr Dosson thought it natural that any one should want to see his daughter was only equalled by the degree to which the young man thought it natural her father should find her for him. There was a superfluous drapery in the doorway of the *salon de lecture*, which Mr

3

Dosson pushed aside while George Flack stepped in after him.

The reading-room of the Hôtel de l'Univers et de Cheltenham was not of great proportions, and had seemed to Mr Dosson from the first to consist principally of a bare, highly-polished floor, on which it was easy for a relaxed elderly American to slip. It was composed further, to his perception, of a table with a green velvet cloth, of a fireplace with a great deal of fringe and no fire, of a window with a great deal of curtain and no light, and of the *Figaro*, which he couldn't read, and the *New York Herald*, which he had already read. A single person was just now in possession of these conveniences—a young lady who sat with her back to the window, looking straight before her into the conventional room. She was dressed as for the street; her empty hands rested upon the arms of her chair (she had withdrawn her long gloves, which were lying in her lap), and she seemed to be doing nothing as hard as she could. Her face was so much in shadow as to be barely distinguishable; nevertheless, as soon as he saw her, the young man exclaimed—'Why, it ain't Miss Francie—it's Miss Delia!'

'Well, I guess we can fix that,' said Mr Dosson, wandering further into the room and drawing his feet over the floor without lifting them. Whatever he did he ever seemed to wander: he had a transitory air, an aspect of weary yet patient non-arrival, even when he sat (as he was capable of sitting for hours) in the court of the inn. As he glanced down at the two newspapers in their desert

4

of green velvet he raised a hopeless, uninterested glass to his eye. 'Delia, my dear, where is your sister?'

Delia made no movement whatever, nor did any expression, so far as could be perceived, pass over her large young face. She only ejaculated, 'Why, Mr Flack, where did you drop from?'

'Well, this is a good place to meet,' her father remarked, as if mildly, and as a mere passing suggestion, to deprecate explanations.

'Any place is good where one meets old friends,' said George Flack, looking also at the newspapers. He examined the date of the American sheet and then put it down. 'Well, how do you like Paris?' he went on to the young lady.

'We quite enjoy it; but of course we're familiar now.'

'Well, I was in hopes I could show you something,' Mr Flack said.

'I guess they've seen most everything,' Mr Dosson observed.

'Well, we've seen more than you!' exclaimed his daughter.

'Well, I've seen a good deal—just sitting there.'

A person with a delicate ear might have suspected Mr Dosson of saying 'setting'; but he would pronounce the same word in a different manner at different times.

'Well, in Paris you can see everything,' said the young man. 'I'm quite enthusiastic about Paris.'

'Haven't you been here before?' Miss Delia asked.

'Oh, yes, but it's ever fresh. And how is Miss Francie?'

'She's all right. She has gone up stairs to get something; we are going out again.'

'It's very attractive for the young,' said Mr Dosson to the visitor.

'Well, then, I'm one of the young. Do you mind if I go with you?' Mr Flack continued, to the girl.

'It'll seem like old times, on the deck,' she replied. 'We're going to the Bon Marché.'

'Why don't you go to the Louvre? It's much better.'

'We have just come from there: we have had quite a morning.'

'Well, it's a good place,' the visitor continued.

'It's good for some things but it doesn't come up to my idea for others.'

'Oh, they've seen everything,' said Mr Dosson. Then he added, 'I guess I'll go and call Francie.'

'Well, tell her to hurry,' Miss Delia returned, swinging a glove in each hand.

'She knows my pace,' Mr Flack remarked.

'I should think she would, the way you raced!' the girl ejaculated, with memories of the Umbria. 'I hope you don't expect to rush round Paris that way.'

'I always rush. I live in a rush. That's the way to get through.'

'Well, I *am* through, I guess,' said Mr Dosson, philosophically.

'Well, I ain't!' his daughter declared with decision.

'Well, you must come round often,' the old gentleman continued, as a leave-taking.

'Oh, I'll come round! I'll have to rush, but I'll do it.'

'I'll send down Francie.' And Francie's father crept away.

'And please to give her some more money!' her sister called after him.

'Does she keep the money?' George Flack inquired.

'*Keep* it?' Mr Dosson stopped as he pushed aside the *portière*. 'Oh, you innocent young man!'

'I guess it's the first time you were ever called innocent,' Delia remarked, left alone with the visitor.

'Well, I *was*—before I came to Paris.'

'Well, I can't see that it has hurt us. We are *not* extravagant.'

'Wouldn't you have a right to be?'

'I don't think any one has a right to be.'

The young man, who had seated himself, looked at her a moment. 'That's the way you used to talk.'

'Well, I haven't changed.'

'And Miss Francie—has she?'

'Well, you'll see,' said Delia Dosson, beginning to draw on her gloves.

Her companion watched her, leaning forward, with his elbows on the arms of his chair and his hands interlocked. At last he said interrogatively: 'Bon Marché?'

'No, I got them in a little place I know.'

'Well, they're Paris, anyway.'

'Of course they're Paris. But you can get gloves anywhere.'

'You must show me the little place, anyhow,' Mr Flack

7

continued, sociably. And he observed further, with the same friendliness—'The old gentleman seems all there.'

'Oh, he's the dearest of the dear.'

'He's a real gentleman—of the old stamp,' said George Flack.

'Well, what should you think our father would be?'

'I should think he would be delighted!'

'Well, he is, when we carry out our plans.'

'And what are they—your plans?' asked the young man.

'Oh, I never tell them.'

'How then does he know whether you carry them out?'

'Well, I guess he'd know it if we didn't,' said the girl.

'I remember how secretive you were last year. You kept everything to yourself.'

'Well, I know what I want,' the young lady pursued.

He watched her button one of her gloves, deftly, with a hairpin which she disengaged from some mysterious function under her bonnet. There was a moment's silence and then they looked up at each other. 'I have an idea you don't want me,' said George Flack.

'Oh, yes, I do—as a friend.'

'Of all the mean ways of trying to get rid of a man, that's the meanest!' he exclaimed.

'Where's the meanness, when I suppose you are not so peculiar as to wish to be anything more!'

'More to your sister, do you mean—or to yourself?'

'My sister *is* myself—I haven't got any other,' said Delia Dosson.

'Any other sister?'

'Don't be idiotic. Are you still in the same business?' the girl went on.

'Well, I forget which one I *was* in.'

'Why, something to do with that newspaper—don't you remember?'

'Yes, but it isn't that paper any more—it's a different one.'

'Do you go round for news—in the same way?'

'Well, I try to get the people what they want. It's hard work,' said the young man.

'Well, I suppose if you didn't someone else would. They will have it, won't they?'

'Yes, they will have it.' But the wants of the people did not appear at the present moment to interest Mr Flack as much as his own. He looked at his watch and remarked that the old gentleman didn't seem to have much authority.

'Much authority?' the girl repeated.

'With Miss Francie. She is taking her time, or rather, I mean, she is taking mine.'

'Well, if you expect to do anything with her you must give her plenty of that.'

'All right: I'll give her all I have.' And Miss Dosson's interlocutor leaned back in his chair with folded arms, as if to let his companion know that she would have to count with his patience. But she sat there in her expressionless placidity, giving no sign of alarm or defeat. He was the first indeed to show a symptom of restlessness: at the end of a few moments he asked the young lady if she didn't suppose her father had told her sister who it was.

'Do you think that's all that's required?' Miss Dosson demanded. But she added, more graciously—'Probably that's the reason. She's so shy.'

'Oh, yes—she used to look it.'

'No, that's her peculiarity, that she never looks it, and yet she is intensely so.'

'Well, you make it up for her then, Miss Delia,' the young man ventured to declare.

'No, for her, I'm not shy—not in the least.'

'If it wasn't for you I think I could do something,' the young man went on.

'Well, you've got to kill me first!'

'I'll come down on you, somehow, in the *Reverberator*,' said George Flack.

'Oh, that's not what the people want.'

'No, unfortunately they don't care anything about *my* affairs.'

'Well, we do: we are kinder, Francie and I,' said the girl. 'But we desire to keep them quite distinct from ours.'

'Oh, yours—yours: if I could only discover what they are!' the young journalist exclaimed. And during the rest of the time that they sat there waiting he tried to find out. If an auditor had happened to be present for the quarter of an hour that elapsed and had had any attention to give to these vulgar young persons he would have wondered perhaps at there being so much mystery on one side and so much curiosity on the other—wondered at least at the elaboration of inscrutable projects on the part of a girl who looked to the casual eye as if she were stolidly passive. Fidelia Dosson, whose name had been shortened, was twenty-five years old and had a large white face, with the eyes very far apart. Her forehead was high, but her mouth was small: her hair was light and colourless, and a certain inelegant thickness of figure made her appear shorter than she was. Elegance indeed had not been conferred upon her by Nature, and the Bon Marché and other establishments had to make up for that. To a feminine eye they would scarcely have appeared to have acquitted themselves of their office; but even a woman would not have guessed how little Fidelia cared. She always looked the same; all the contrivances of Paris could not make her look different, and she held them, for herself, in no manner of esteem. It was a plain, blank face, not only without movement, but with a suggestion of obstinacy in its repose; and yet, with its limitations, it was neither stupid nor displeasing. It had an air of intelligent calm—a considering, pondering look that was superior, somehow, to diffidence, or anxiety; moreover, the girl had a clear skin and a gentle, dim smile. If she had been a young man (and she had, a little, the head of one) it would probably have been thought of her that she nursed dreams of eminence in some scientific or even political line.

An observer would have gathered, further, that Mr Flack's acquaintance with Mr Dosson and his daughters had had its origin in his crossing the Atlantic eastward in their company more than a year before and in some slight association immediately after disembarking; but that each party had come and gone a good deal since then—come and gone however without meeting again. It was to be inferred that in this interval Miss Dosson had led her father and sister back to their native land and had then a second time directed their course to Europe. This was a new departure, said Mr Flack, or rather a new arrival: he understood that it was not, as he called it, the same old visit. She did not repudiate the accusation, launched by her companion as if it might have been embarrassing, of having spent her time at home in Boston, and even in a suburban portion of it: she confessed that, as Bostonians, they had been capable of that. But now they had come abroad for longer—ever so much: what they had gone home for was to make arrangements for a European sojourn of which the limits were not to be told. So far as this prospect entered into her plans she freely acknowledged it. It appeared to meet with George Flack's approval—he also had a big job on that side and it might take years, so that it would be pleasant to have his friends right there. He knew his way about in Paris—or any place like that—much more than in Boston; if they had been poked away in one of those clever suburbs they would have been lost to him.

'Oh, well, you'll see as much as you want to of us— the way you'll have to take us,' Delia Dosson said: which led the young man to inquire what way that was and to remark that he only knew one way to take anything— just as it came. 'Oh, well, you'll see,' the girl rejoined; and she would give for the present no further explanation of her somewhat chilling speech. In spite of it however she professed an interest in Mr Flack's 'job'—an interest which rested apparently upon an interest in the young man himself. The slightly surprised observer whom we have supposed to be present would have perceived that this latter sentiment was founded on a conception of Mr Flack's intrinsic brilliancy. Would his own impression have justified that?—would he have found such a conception contagious? I forbear to say positively no, for that would charge me with the large responsibility of showing what right our accidental observer might have had to his particular standard. I prefer therefore to note simply that George Flack was quite clever enough to seem a person of importance to Delia Dosson. He was connected (as she supposed) with literature, and was not literature one of the many engaging attributes of her cherished little sister? If Mr Flack was a writer Francie was a reader: had not a trail of forgotten Tauchnitzes marked the former line of travel of the party of three? The elder sister grabbed them up on leaving hotels and railway-carriages, but usually found that she had brought odd volumes. She considered however that as a family they had a sort of superior affinity with the young journalist, and would have been surprised if she had been told that his acquaintance was not a high advantage.

Mr Flack's appearance was not so much a property of his own as a prejudice on the part of those who looked at him: whoever they might be what they saw mainly in him was that they had seen him before. And, oddly enough, this recognition carried with it in general no ability to remember—that is to recall—him: you could not have evoked him in advance, and it was only when you saw him that you knew you *had* seen him. To carry him in your mind you must have liked him very much, for no other sentiment, not even aversion, would have taught you what distinguished him in his group: aversion in especial would have made you conscious only of what confounded him. He was not a particular person, but a sample or memento—reminding one of certain 'goods' for which there is a steady popular demand. You would scarcely have expected him to have a name other than that of his class: a number, like that of the day's newspaper, would have been the most that you would count on, and you would have expected vaguely to find the number high—somewhere up in the millions. As every copy of the newspaper wears the same label, so that of Miss Dosson's visitor would have been 'Young commercial American'. Let me add that among the accidents of his appearance was that of its sometimes striking other young commercial Americans as fine. He was twenty-seven years of age and had a small square head, a light gray overcoat, and in his right fore-finger a curious natural crook which might have served, under pressure, to identify him. But for the convenience of society he ought always to have worn something conspicuous—a green hat or a scarlet necktie. His job was to obtain material in Europe for an American 'society-paper'.

If it be objected to all this that when Francie Dosson at last came in she addressed him as if she easily placed him, the answer is that she had been notified by her father —more punctually than was indicated by the manner of her response. 'Well, the way you *do* turn up,' she said, smiling and holding out her left hand to him: in the other hand, or the hollow of her right arm, she had a largeish parcel. Though she had made him wait she was evidently very glad to see him there; and she as evidently required, and enjoyed, a great deal of that sort of indulgence. Her sister's attitude would have told you so even if her own appearance had not. There was that in her manner to the young man—a perceptible but indefinable shade—which seemed to legitimate the oddity of his having asked in particular for her, as if he wished to see her to the exclusion of her father and sister: a kind of special pleasure which had the air of pointing to a special relation. And yet a spectator, looking from Mr George Flack to Miss Francie Dosson, would have been much at a loss to guess what special relation could exist between them. The girl was exceedingly, extraordinarily pretty, and without discoverable resemblance to her sister; and there was a brightness in her—a kind of still radiance—which was quite distinct from what is called animation. Rather tall than short, slim, delicate and evidently as light of hand and of foot as it was possible to be, she yet gave no impression of quick movement, of abundant chatter, of excitable nerves and irrepressible life—no hint of being of the most usual (which is perhaps also the most graceful) American type. She was brilliantly but quietly pretty, and your suspicion that she was a little stiff was corrected only by your perception that she was extremely soft. There was nothing in her to confirm the implication that she had rushed about the deck of a Cunarder with a news-paper-man. She was as straight as a wand and as fine as a gem; her neck was long and her gray eyes had colour; and from the ripple of her dark brown hair to the curve of her unaffirmative chin every line in her face was happy and pure. She had an unformed voice and very little knowledge.

Delia got up, and they came out of the little reading-room—this young lady remarking to her sister that she hoped she had got all the things. 'Well, I had a fiendish hunt for them, we have got so many,' Francie replied, with a curious soft drawl. 'There were a few dozens of the pocket-handkerchiefs I couldn't find; but I guess I've got most of them, and most of the gloves.'

'Well, what are you carting them about for?' George Flack inquired, taking the parcel from her. 'You had better let me handle them. Do you buy pocket-handker-chiefs by the hundred?'

'Well, it only makes fifty apiece,' said Francie, smiling. 'They ain't nice—we're going to change them.'

'Oh, I won't be mixed up with that—you can't work that game on these Frenchmen!' the young man ex-claimed.

'Oh, with Francie they will take anything back,' Delia Dosson declared. 'They just love her, all over.'

'Well, they're like me then,' said Mr Flack, with friendly hilarity. 'I'll take her back, if she'll come.'

'Well, I don't think I am ready quite yet,' the girl replied. 'But I hope very much we shall cross with you again.'

'Talk about crossing—it's on these boulevards we want a life-preserver!' Delia remarked. They had passed out of the hotel and the wide vista of the Rue de la Paix stretched up and down. There were many vehicles.

'Won't this thing do? I'll tie it to either of you,' George Flack said, holding out his bundle. 'I suppose they won't kill you if they love you,' he went on, to the younger girl.

'Well, you've got to know me first,' she answered, laughing and looking for a chance, while they waited to pass over.

'I didn't know you when I was struck.' He applied his disengaged hand to her elbow and propelled her across the street. She took no notice of his observation, and Delia asked her, on the other side, whether their father had given her that money. She replied that he had given her loads—she felt as if he had made his will; which led George Flack to say that he wished the old gentleman was *his* father.

'Why, you don't mean to say you want to be our brother!' Francie exclaimed, as they went down the Rue de la Paix.

'I should like to be Miss Delia's, if you can make that out,' said the young man.

'Well, then, suppose you prove it by calling me a cab,' Miss Delia returned. 'I presume you and Francie don't think this is the deck.'

'Don't she feel rich?' George Flack demanded of Francie. 'But we do require a cart for our goods;' and he hailed a little yellow carriage, which presently drew up beside the pavement. The three got into it and, still emitting innocent pleasantries, proceeded on their way, while at the Hôtel de l'Univers et de Cheltenham Mr Dosson wandered down into the court again and took his place in his customary chair.

II

THE court was roofed with glass; the April air was mild; the cry of women selling violets came in from the street and, mingling with the rich hum of Paris, seemed to bring with it faintly the odour of the flowers. There were other odours in the place, warm, succulent and Parisian, which ranged from fried fish to burnt sugar; and there were many things besides: little tables for the post-prandial coffee; piles of luggage inscribed (after the initials, or frequently the name, R. P. Scudamore or D. Jackson Hatch), Philadelphia, Pa., or St Louis, Mo.; rattles of unregarded bells, flittings of tray-bearing waiters, conversations with the second-floor windows of admonitory landladies, arrivals of young women with coffinlike bandboxes covered with black oilcloth and depending from a strap, sallyings forth of persons staying and arrivals, just afterwards, of other persons to see them; together with vague prostrations on benches of tired heads of American families. It was to this last element that Mr Dosson himself in some degree contributed, but it must be added that he had not the extremely bereft and exhausted appearance of certain of his fellows. There was an air of meditative patience, of habitual accommodation in him; but you would have guessed that he was enjoying a holiday rather than panting for a truce, and he was not so enfeebled but that he was able to get up from time to time and stroll through the *porte cochère* to have a look at the street.

He gazed up and down for five minutes, with his hands in his pockets, and then came back; that appeared to content him; he asked for very little—had no restlessness that these small excursions would not assuage. He looked at the heaped-up luggage, at the tinkling bells, at the young woman from the *lingère*, at the repudiated visitors, at everything but the other American parents. Something in his breast told him that he knew all about these. It is not upon each other that the animals in the same cage, in a zoological collection, most turn their eyes. There was a silent sociability in him and a superficial fineness of grain that helped to account for his daughter Francie's various delicacies. He was fair and spare and had no figure; you would have seen in a moment that the question of how he should hold himself had never in his life occurred to him. He never held himself at all; providence held him rather (and very loosely), by an invisible string, at the end

of which he seemed gently to dangle and waver. His face
was so smooth that his thin light whiskers, which grew
only far back, scarcely seemed native to his cheeks: they
might have been attached there for some harmless purpose of comedy or disguise. He looked for the most part
as if he were thinking over, without exactly understanding it, something rather droll which had just occurred; if
his eyes wandered his attention rested, and hurried, quite
as little. His feet were remarkably small, and his clothes,
in which light colours predominated, were visibly the
work of a French tailor: he was an American who still
held the tradition that it is in Paris a man dresses himself
best. His hat would have looked odd in Bond Street or
the Fifth Avenue, and his necktie was loose and flowing.

Mr Dosson, it may further be mentioned, was a man
of the simplest composition, a character as cipherable as a
sum of two figures. He had a native financial faculty of the
finest order, a gift as direct as a beautiful tenor voice,
which had enabled him, without the aid of particular
strength of will or keenness of ambition, to build up a
large fortune while he was still of middle age. He had a
genius for happy speculation, the quick, unerring instinct
of a 'good thing'; and as he sat there idle, amused, con-
tented, on the edge of the Parisian street, he might very
well have passed for some rare performer who had sung
his song or played his trick and had nothing to do till
the next call. And he had grown rich not because he was
ravenous or hard, but simply because he had an ear, or a
nose. He could make out the tune in the discord of the

market-place; he could smell success far up the wind. The second factor in his little addition was that he was an un-assuming father. He had no tastes, no acquirements nor curiosities, and his daughters represented society for him. He thought much more and much oftener of these young ladies than of his bank-shares and railway-stock; they refreshed much more his sense of ownership, of accumulation. He never compared them with other girls; he only compared his present self to what he would have been without them. His view of them was perfectly simple. Delia had a more unfathomable profundity and Francie a wider acquaintance with literature and art. Mr Dosson had not perhaps a full perception of his younger daughter's beauty: he would scarcely have pretended to judge of that, more than he would of a valuable picture or vase, but he believed she was cultivated up to the eyes. He had a recollection of tremendous school-bills and, in later days, during their travels, of the way she was always leaving books behind her. Moreover was not her French so good that he could not understand it?

The two girls, at any rate, were the wind in his sail and the only directing, determining force he knew; they converted accident into purpose; without them, as he felt, he would have been the tail without the kite. The wind rose and fell, of course; there were lulls and there were gales; there were intervals during which he simply floated in quiet waters—cast anchor and waited. This appeared to be one of them now; but he could be patient, knowing that he should soon again inhale the brine and feel the

dip of his prow. When his daughters were out the determining process gathered force, and their being out with a
brilliant young man only deepened the pleasant calm.
That belonged to their superior life, and Mr Dosson
never doubted that George M. Flack was brilliant. He
represented the newspaper, and the newspaper for this
man of genial assumptions represented Mind—it was the
great shining presence of our time. To know that Delia
and Francie were out with an editor or a correspondent
was really to see them dancing in the central glow. This
is doubtless why Mr Dosson had slightly more than usual
his air of recovering slowly from a pleasant surprise. The
vision to which I allude hung before him, at a convenient
distance, and melted into other bright confused aspects:
reminiscences of Mr Flack in other relations—on the
ship, on the deck, at the hotel at Liverpool, and in the
cars. Whitney Dosson was a loyal father, but he would
have thought himself simple had he not had two
or three strong convictions: one of which was that
the children should never go out with a gentleman
they had not seen before. The sense of their having, and
his having, seen Mr Flack before was comfortable to him
now: it made it mere placidity for him personally to fore-
go the young man's society in favour of Delia and Francie. He had not hitherto been perfectly satisfied that the
streets and shops, the general immensity of Paris, were
just the right place for young ladies alone. But the company of a pleasant gentleman made them right—a gentleman who was pleasant through being up to everything, as

one connected with that paper (he remembered its name now, it was celebrated) would have to be. To Mr Dosson, in the absence of such happy accidents, his girls somehow seemed lonely; which was not the way he struck himself. They were his company but he was scarcely theirs; it was as if he had them more than they had him.

They were out a long time, but he felt no anxiety, as he reflected that Mr Flack's very profession was a prevision of everything that could possibly happen. The bright French afternoon waned without bringing them back, but Mr Dosson still revolved about the court, till he might have been taken for a *valet de place* hoping to pick up custom. The landlady smiled at him sometimes, as she passed and re-passed, and even ventured to remark disinterestedly that it was a pity to waste such a lovely day indoors—not to take a turn and see what was going on in Paris. But Mr Dosson had no sense of waste: that came to him much more when he was confronted with historical monuments, or beauties of nature or art, which he didn't understand nor care for: then he felt a little ashamed and uncomfortable—but never when he lounged in that simplifying way in the court. It wanted but a quarter of an hour to dinner (that he could understand) when Delia and Francie at last met his view, still accompanied by Mr Flack and sauntering in, at a little distance from each other, with a jaded air which was not in the least a tribute to his possible solicitude. They dropped into chairs and joked with each other, with a mixture of sociability and languor, on the subject of what they had

seen and done—a question into which he felt as yet a
delicacy as to inquiring. But they had evidently done a
good deal and had a good time: an impression sufficient
to rescue Mr Dosson personally from the consciousness
of failure.

'Won't you just step in and take dinner with us?' he
asked of the young man, with a friendliness begotten of
the circumstances.

'Well, that's a handsome offer,' George Flack replied,
while Delia remarked that they had each eaten about
thirty cakes.

'Well, I wondered what you were doing so long. But
never mind your cakes. It's twenty minutes past six, and
the *table d'hôte* is on time.'

'You don't mean to say you dine at the *table d'hôte*!'
Mr Flack ejaculated.

'Why, don't you like that?' Francie drawled sweetly.

'Well, it isn't what you most build on when you come
to Paris. Too many flower-pots and chickens' legs.'

'Well, would you like one of these restaurants?' asked
Mr Dosson. 'I don't care, if you show us a good one.'

'Oh, I'll show you a good one—don't you worry.'

'Well, you've got to order the dinner then,' said
Francie.

'Well, you'll see how I could do it!' And the young
man looked at her very hard, with an intention of softness.

'He has got an interest in some place,' Delia declared.
'He has taken us to ever so many stores, and he gets his
commission.'

'Well, I'd pay you to take them round,' said Mr Dosson; and with much agreeable trifling of this kind it was agreed that they should sally forth for the evening meal under Mr Flack's guidance.

If he had easily convinced them on this occasion that that was a more original proceeding than worrying those old bones, as he called it, at the hotel, he convinced them of other things besides in the course of the following month and by the aid of repeated visits. What he mainly made clear to them was that it was really most kind of a young man who had so many great public questions on his mind to find sympathy for problems which could fill the telegraph and the press so little as theirs. He came every day to set them in the right path, pointing out its charms to them in a way that made them feel how much they had been in the wrong. He made them feel indeed that they didn't know anything about anything, even about such a matter as ordering shoes—an art in which they vaguely supposed themselves rather strong. He had in fact great knowledge, and it was wonderfully various, and he knew as many people as they knew few. He had appointments—very often with celebrities—for every hour of the day, and memoranda, sometimes in shorthand, on tablets with elastic straps, with which he dazzled the simple folk at the Hôtel de l'Univers et de Cheltenham, whose social life, of narrow range, consisted mainly in reading the lists of Americans who 'registered' at the bankers' and at Galignani's. Delia Dosson, in particular, had a way of poring solemnly over these records which exasperated Mr Flack, who skimmed them and found what he wanted in the flash of an eye: she kept the others waiting while she satisfied herself that Mr and Mrs D. S. Rosenheim and Miss Cora Rosenheim and Master Samuel Rosenheim had 'left for Brussels'.

Mr Flack was wonderful on all occasions in finding what he wanted (which, as we know, was what he believed the public wanted), and Delia was the only one of the party with whom he was sometimes a little sharp. He had embraced from the first the idea that she was his enemy, and he alluded to it with almost tiresome frequency, though always in a humorous, fearless strain. Even more than by her fashion of hanging over the registers she provoked him by appearing to think that their little party was not sufficient to itself; by wishing, as he expressed it, to work in new stuff. He might have been easy, however, for he had sufficient chance to observe how it was always the fate of the Dossons to miss their friends. They were continually looking out for meetings and combinations that never came off, hearing that people had been in Paris only after they had gone away, or feeling convinced that they were there but not to be found through their not having registered, or wondering whether they should overtake them if they should go to Dresden, and then making up their minds to start for Dresden, only to learn, at the eleventh hour, through some accident, that the elusive party had gone to Biarritz. 'We know plenty of people if we could only come across them,' Delia had said more than once: she scanned the continent with a wondering, baffled gaze and talked of the unsatisfactory way in which friends at home would 'write out' that other friends were 'somewhere in Europe'. She expressed the wish that such correspondents as that might be in a place that was not at all vague. Two or three times people had called at the hotel when they were out and had left cards for them, without any address, superscribed with a mocking dash of the pencil, 'Off to-morrow!' The girl sat looking at these cards, handling them and turning them over for a quarter of an hour at a time; she produced them days afterwards, brooding upon them afresh as if they were a mystic clue. George Flack generally knew where they were, the people who were 'somewhere in Europe'. Such knowledge came to him by a kind of intuition, by the voices of the air, by indefinable and unteachable processes. But he held his peace on purpose; he didn't want any outsiders; he thought their little party just right. Mr Dosson's place in the scheme of providence was to go with Delia while he himself went with Francie, and nothing would have induced George Flack to disfigure that equation.

The young man was professionally so occupied with other people's affairs that it should doubtless be mentioned to his praise that he still managed to have affairs— or at least an affair—of his own. That affair was Francie Dosson, and he was pleased to perceive how little *she* cared what had become of Mr and Mrs Rosenheim and Master Samuel and Miss Cora. He counted all the things she didn't care about—her soft inadvertent eyes helped him to do that; and they footed up so, as he would have said, that they gave him a pleasant sense of a free field. If she had so few interests there was the greater possibility that a young man of bold conceptions and cheerful manners might become one. She had usually the air of waiting for something, with a sort of amused resignation, while tender, shy, indefinite little fancies hummed in her brain; so that she would perhaps recognise in him the reward of patience. George Flack was aware that he exposed his friends to considerable fatigue; he brought them back pale and taciturn from suburban excursions, and from wanderings, often rather aimless and casual, among the boulevards and avenues of the town. He regarded them at such moments with complacency however, for these were hours of diminished resistance: he had an idea that he should be able eventually to circumvent Delia if he could only watch for some time when she was tired. He liked to make them all feel helpless and dependent, and this was not difficult with people who were so modest and artless, so unconscious of the boundless power of wealth. Sentiment, in our young man, was not a scruple nor a source of weakness; but he thought it really touching, the little these good people knew of what they could do with their money. They had in their hands a weapon of infinite range and yet they were incapable of firing a shot for themselves. They had a kind of social humility; it appeared never to have occurred to them that, added to their amiability, their money gave them a value. This used to strike George Flack on certain occasions when he came back to find them in the places where he had dropped them while he rushed off to give a turn to one of his screws. They never played him false, never wearied of waiting; always sat patient and submissive, usually at a café to which he had introduced them or in a row of chairs on the boulevard, or in the Tuileries or the Champs Elysées.

He introduced them to many cafés, in different parts of Paris, being careful to choose those which (in his view) young ladies might frequent with propriety, and there were two or three in the neighbourhood of their hotel where they became frequent and familiar figures. As the late spring days grew warmer and brighter they usually sat outside on the 'terrace'—the little expanse of small tables at the door of the establishment, where Mr Flack, on the return, could descry them from afar at their post in exactly the same position to which he had committed them. They complained of no satiety in watching the many-coloured movement of the Parisian streets: and if some of the features in the panorama were base they were only so in a version which the imagination of our friends was incapable of supplying. George Flack considered that he was rendering a positive service to Mr Dosson: wouldn't the old gentleman have sat all day in the court anyway? and wasn't the boulevard better than the court? It was his theory too that he flattered and caressed Miss Francie's father, for there was no one to whom he had furnished more copious details about the affairs, the projects and prospects, of the *Reverberator*. He had left no doubt in the old gentleman's mind as to the race he himself intended to run, and Mr Dosson used to say to him every day, the first thing, 'Well, where have you got to now?' as if he took a real interest. George Flack narrated his interviews, to which Delia and Francie gave attention only in case they knew something of the persons on whom the young emissary of the *Reverberator* had conferred this distinction; whereas Mr Dosson listened, with his tolerant interposition of 'Is that so?' and 'Well, that's good', just as submissively when he heard of the celebrity in question for the first time.

In conversation with his daughters Mr Flack was frequently the theme, though introduced much more by the young ladies than by himself, and especially by Delia, who announced at an early period that she knew what he wanted and that it wasn't in the least what *she* wanted. She amplified this statement very soon—at least as regards her interpretation of Mr Flack's designs: a certain mystery still hung about her own, which, as she intimated, had much more to recommend them. Delia's vision of the danger as well as the advantage of being a pretty girl was closely connected (and this was natural) with the idea of an 'engagement': this idea was in a manner complete in itself—her imagination failed in the oddest way to carry it into the next stage. She wanted her sister to be engaged but she wanted her not at all to be married, and she had not clearly made up her mind as to how Francie was to enjoy both the promotion and the arrest. It was a secret source of humiliation to her that there had as yet to her knowledge been no one with

whom her sister had exchanged vows; if her conviction
on this subject could have expressed itself intelligibly it
would have given you a glimpse of a droll state of mind—
a dim theory that a bright girl ought to be able to try
successive aspirants. Delia's conception of what such a
trial might consist of was strangely innocent: it was made
up of calls and walks and buggy-drives and above all of
being spoken of as engaged; and it never occurred to her
that a repetition of lovers rubs off a young lady's delicacy.
She felt herself a born old maid and never dreamed of a
lover of her own—he would have been dreadfully in her
way; but she dreamed of love as something in its nature
very delicate. All the same she discriminated; it did lead
to something after all, and she desired that for Francie it
should not lead to a union with Mr Flack. She looked at
such a union in the light of that other view which she
kept as yet to herself but which she was ready to produce
so soon as the right occasion should come up; and she
told her sister that she would never speak to her again
if she should let this young man suppose—— And here
she always paused, plunging again into impressive
reticence.

'Suppose what?' Francie asked, as if she were totally
unacquainted (which indeed she really was) with the sup-
positions of young men.

'Well, you'll see, when he begins to say things you
won't like.' This sounded ominous on Delia's part, but
she had in reality very little apprehension; otherwise she
would have risen against the custom adopted by Mr

Flack of perpetually coming round: she would have given her attention (though it struggled in general unsuccessfully with all this side of their life) to some prompt means of getting away from Paris. She told her father what in her view the correspondent of the *Reverberator* was 'after'; but it must be added that she did not make him feel very strongly on the matter. This however was not of importance, with her inner sense that Francie would never really do anything—that is would never really like anything—they didn't like.

Her sister's docility was a great comfort to her, especially as it was addressed in the first instance to herself. She liked and disliked certain things much more than the younger girl did either; and Francie was glad to take advantage of her reasons, having so few of her own. They served—Delia's reasons—for Mr Dosson as well, so that Francie was not guilty of any particular irreverence in regarding her sister rather than her father as the controller of her fate. A fate was rather a cumbersome and formidable possession, which it relieved her that some kind person should undertake the keeping of. Delia had somehow got hold of hers first—before even her father, and ever so much before Mr Flack; and it lay with Delia to make any change. She could not have accepted any gentleman as a husband without reference to Delia, any more than she could have done up her hair without a glass. The only action taken by Mr Dosson in consequence of his elder daughter's revelations was to embrace the idea as a subject of daily pleasantry. He was fond, in his intercourse with his children, of some small usual joke, some humorous refrain; and what could have been more in the line of true domestic sport than a little gentle but unintermitted raillery upon Francie's conquest? Mr Flack's attributive intentions became a theme of indulgent parental chaff, and the girl was neither dazzled nor annoyed by such familiar references to them. 'Well, he *has* told us about half we know,' she used often to reply.

Among the things he told them was that this was the very best time in the young lady's life to have her portrait painted and the best place in the world to have it done well; also that he knew a 'lovely artist', a young American of extraordinary talent, who would be delighted to undertake the work. He conducted them to this gentleman's studio, where they saw several pictures by which they were considerably mystified. Francie protested that she didn't want to be done *that* way, and Delia declared that she would as soon have her sister shown up in a magic lantern. They had had the fortune not to find Mr Waterlow at home, so that they were free to express themselves and the pictures were shown them by his servant. They looked at them as they looked at bonnets and *confections* when they went to expensive shops; as if it were a question, among so many specimens, of the style and colour they would choose. Mr Waterlow's productions struck them for the most part in the same manner as those garments which ladies classify as frights, and they went away with a very low opinion of the young

American master. George Flack told them however that they couldn't get out of it, inasmuch as he had already written home to the *Reverberator* that Francie was to sit. They accepted this somehow as a kind of supernatural sign that she would have to; for they believed everything that they heard quoted from a newspaper. Moreover Mr Flack explained to them that it would be idiotic to miss such an opportunity to get something at once precious and cheap; for it was well known that Impressionism was going to be the art of the future, and Charles Waterlow was a rising Impressionist. It was a new system altogether and the latest improvement in art. They didn't want to go back, they wanted to go forward, and he would give them an article that would fetch five times the money in a couple of years. They were not in search of a bargain, but they allowed themselves to be inoculated with any reason which they thought would be characteristic of earnest people; and he even convinced them, after a little, that when once they had got used to Impressionism they would never look at anything else. Mr Waterlow was *the* man, among the young, and he had no interest in praising him, because he was not a personal friend; his reputation was advancing with strides, and any one with any sense would want to secure something before the rush.

III

THE young ladies consented to return to the Avenue de Villiers, and this time they found the celebrity of the future. He was smoking cigarettes with a friend, while coffee was served to the two gentlemen (it was just after luncheon), on a vast divan, covered with scrappy oriental rugs and cushions; it looked, Francie thought, as if the artist had set up a carpet-shop in a corner. She thought him very pleasant; and it may be mentioned without circumlocution that the young lady ushered in by the vulgar American reporter, whom he didn't like and who had already come too often to his studio to pick up 'glimpses' (the painter wondered how in the world he had picked *her* up), this charming candidate for portraiture struck Charles Waterlow on the spot as an adorable model. She made, it may further be declared, quite the same impression on the gentleman who was with him and who never took his eyes off her while her own rested, afresh, on several finished and unfinished canvases. This gentleman asked of his friend, at the end of five minutes, the favour of an introduction to her; in consequence of which Francie learned that his name (she thought it singular) was Gaston Probert. Mr Probert was a kind-eyed, smiling youth, who fingered the points of his moustache; he was represented by Mr Waterlow as an American, but he pronounced the American language (so at least it seemed to Francie) as if it had been French.

After Francie had quitted the studio with Delia and Mr Flack (her father, on this occasion, was not of the party), the two young men, falling back upon their divan, broke into expressions of æsthetic rapture, declared that the girl had qualities—oh, but qualities, and a charm of line! They remained there for an hour, contemplating these rare properties in the smoke of their cigarettes. You would have gathered from their conversation (though as regards much of it only perhaps with the aid of a grammar and dictionary) that the young lady possessed plastic treasures of the highest order, of which she was evidently quite unconscious. Before this however Mr Waterlow had come to an understanding with his visitors—it had been settled that Miss Francina should sit for him at his first hour of leisure. Unfortunately that hour presented itself as still remote and he was unable to make a definite appointment. He had sitters on his hands—he had at least three portraits to finish before going to Spain. And he adverted with bitterness to the journey to Spain—a little excursion laid out precisely with his friend Probert for the last weeks of the spring, the first of the southern summer, the time of the long days and the real light. Gaston Probert re-echoed his regrets, for though he had no business with Miss Francina (he liked her name), he also wanted to see her again. They half agreed to give up Spain (they had, after all, been there before), so that Waterlow might take the girl in hand without delay, the moment he had knocked off his present work. This amendment did not hold however, for other considerations came up and the artist resigned himself to the arrangement on which the Miss Dossons had quitted him: he thought it so characteristic of their nationality that they should settle a matter of that sort for themselves. This was simply that they should come back in the autumn, when he should be comparatively free: then there would be a margin and they might all take their time. At present, before long (by the time he should be ready), the question of Miss Francina's leaving Paris for the summer would be sure to come up, and that would be a tiresome interruption. She liked Paris, she had no plans for the autumn and only wanted a reason to come back about the twentieth of September. Mr Waterlow remarked humorously that she evidently bossed the shop. Meanwhile, before starting for Spain, he would see her as often as possible—his eye would take possession of her.

His companion envied him his eye; he intimated that he was jealous of his eye. It was perhaps as a step towards establishing his right to be jealous that Mr Probert left a card upon the Miss Dossons at the Hôtel de l'Univers et de Cheltenham, having first ascertained that such a proceeding would not, by the young American sisters, be regarded as an unwarrantable liberty. Gaston Probert was an American who had never been in America, and he was obliged to take counsel on such an emergency as that. He knew that in Paris young men did not call at hotels on honourable damsels; but he also knew that honourable damsels did not visit young men in studios;

and he had no guide, no light that he could trust, save the wisdom of his friend Waterlow, which however was for the most part communicated to him in a derisive and misleading form. Waterlow, who was after all himself an ornament of the French, and the very French, school, jeered at his want of national instinct, at the way he never knew by which end to take hold of a compatriot. Poor Probert was obliged to confess that he had had terribly little practice, and in the great medley of aliens and brothers (and even more of sisters), he couldn't tell which was which. He would have had a country and country-men, to say nothing of countrywomen, if he could; but that matter had not been settled for him and there is a difficulty in settling it for one's self. Born in Paris, he had been brought up altogether on French lines, in a family which French society had irrecoverably absorbed. His father, a Carolinian and a Catholic, was a Gallo-maniac of the old American type. His three sisters had married Frenchmen, and one of them lived in Brittany and the others much of the time in Touraine. His only brother had fallen, during the terrible year, in defence of their adoptive country. Yet Gaston, though he had had an old Legitimist marquis for his godfather, was not legally one of its children; his mother had, on her death-bed, extorted from him the promise that he would not take service in its armies; she considered, after the death of her elder son (Gaston, in 1870, was a boy of ten), that the family had been patriotic enough for courtesy.

The young man therefore, between two stools, had no

clear sitting-place: he wanted to be as American as he could and yet not less French than he was; he was afraid to give up the little that he was and find that what he might be was less—he shrank from a flying leap which might drop him in the middle of the sea. At the same time he was aware that the only way to know how it feels to be an American is to try it, and he had many a purpose of making the westward journey. His family however had been so completely Gallicised that the affairs of each member of it were the affairs of all the rest, and his father, his sisters and his brothers-in-law had not yet sufficiently made this scheme their own for him to feel that it was really his. It was a family in which there was no individual but only a collective property. Meanwhile he tried, as I say, by safer enterprises, and especially by going a good deal to see Charles Waterlow in the Avenue de Villiers, whom he believed to be his dearest friend, formed for his affection by Monsieur Carolus. He had an idea that in this manner he kept himself in touch with his countrymen; and he thought he tried especially when he left that card on the Misses Dosson. He was in search of freshness, but he need not have gone far: he need only have turned his lantern upon his own young breast to find a considerable store of it. Like many unoccupied young men at the present hour he gave much attention to art, lived as much as possible in that alternative world, where leisure and vagueness are so mercifully relieved of their crudity. To make up for his want of talent he espoused the talent of others (that is, of several), and was as sensitive and conscientious about them as he might have been about himself. He defended certain of Waterlow's purples and greens as he would have defended his own honour; and in regard to two or three other painters had convictions which belonged almost to the undiscussable part of life. He had not in general a high sense of success, but what kept it down particularly was his indocile hand, the fact that, such as they were, Waterlow's purples and greens, for instance, were far beyond him. If he had not failed there other failures would not have mattered, not even that of not having a country; and it was on the occasion of his friend's agreement to paint that strange, lovely girl, whom he liked so much and whose companions he failed to like, that he felt supremely without a vocation. Freshness was there at least, if he had only had the method. He prayed earnestly, in relation to methods, for a providential reinforcement of Waterlow's sense of this quality. If Waterlow had a fault it was that he was sometimes a little stale.

He avenged himself for the artist's bewildering treatment of his first attempt to approach Miss Francie by indulging, at the end of another week, in a second. He went about six o'clock, when he supposed she would have returned from her day's wanderings, and his prudence was rewarded by the sight of the young lady sitting in the court of the hotel with her father and sister. Mr Dosson was new to Gaston Probert, but the visitor's intelligence embraced him. The little party was as usual expecting Mr Flack at any moment, and they had collected down stairs, so that he might pick them up easily. They had, on the first floor, an expensive parlour, decorated in white and gold, with sofas of crimson damask; but there was something lonely in that grandeur and the place had become mainly a receptacle for their tall trunks, with a half-emptied paper of chocolates or *marrons glacés* on every table. After young Probert's first call his name was often on the lips of the simple trio, and Mr Dosson grew still more jocose, making nothing of a secret of his perception that Francie hit the bull's-eye 'every time'. Mr Waterlow had returned their visit, but that was rather a matter of course, because it was they who had gone after him. They had not gone after the other one; it was he who had come after them. When he entered the hotel, as they sat there, this pursuit and its probable motive became startlingly vivid.

Delia had taken the matter much more gravely than her father; she said there was a great deal she wanted to find out. She mused upon these mysteries visibly, but without advancing much, and she appealed for assistance to George Flack, with a candour which he appreciated and returned. If he knew anything he ought to know who Mr Probert was; and she spoke as if it would be in the natural course that he should elicit the revelation by an interview. Mr Flack promised to 'nose round'; he said the best plan would be that the results should 'come back' to her in the *Reverberator*; he appeared to think that the people could be persuaded that they wanted about a column on Mr Probert. His researches however were fruitless, for in spite of the one fact the girl was able to give him as a starting-point, the fact that their new acquaintance had spent his whole life in Paris, the young journalist couldn't scare up a single person who had even heard of him. He had questioned up and down and all over the place, from the Rue Scribe to the far end of Chaillot, and he knew people who knew others who knew every member of the American colony; that select body which haunted poor Delia's imagination, glittered and re-echoed there in a hundred tormenting roundabout glimpses. That was where she wanted to get Francie, as she said to herself; she wanted to get her right in there. She believed the members of this society to constitute a little kingdom of the blest; and she used to drive through the Avenue Gabriel, the Rue de Marignan and the wide vistas which radiate from the Arch of Triumph and are always changing their names, on purpose to send up wistful glances to the windows (she had learned that all this was the happy quarter) of the enviable but un-approachable colonists. She saw these privileged mortals, as she supposed, in almost every victoria that made a languid lady with a pretty head flash past her, and she had no idea how little honour this theory sometimes did her expatriated countrywomen. Her plan was already made to be on the field again the next winter and take it up seriously, this question of getting Francie in.

When Mr Flack said to her that young Probert's set couldn't be either the rose or anything near it, since the oldest inhabitant had never heard of them, Delia had a flash of inspiration, an intellectual flight that she herself did not measure at the time. She asked if that did not perhaps prove on the contrary quite the opposite—that they were just *the* cream and beyond all others. Was there not a kind of inner circle, and were they not somewhere in the centre of that? George Flack almost quivered at this pregnant suggestion from so unusual a quarter, for he guessed on the spot that Delia Dosson had divined. 'Why, do you mean one of those families that have worked down so far you can't find where they went in?' that was the phrase in which he recognised the truth of the girl's idea. Delia's fixed eyes assented, and after a moment of cogitation George Flack broke out—'That's the kind of family we want a sketch of!'

'Well, perhaps they don't want to be sketched. You had better find out,' Delia had rejoined.

The chance to find out might have seemed to present itself when Mr Probert walked in that confiding way into the hotel; for his arrival was followed, a quarter of an hour later, by that of the representative of the *Reverberator*. Gaston liked the way they treated him; though demonstrative it was not artificial. Mr Dosson said they had been hoping he would come round again, and Delia remarked that she supposed he had had quite a journey— Paris was so big; and she urged his acceptance of a glass of wine or a cup of tea. She added that that wasn't the place where they usually received (she liked to hear herself talk of 'receiving'), and led the party up to her white and gold saloon, where they should be so much more private: she liked also to hear herself talk of privacy. They sat on the red silk chairs and she hoped Mr Probert would at least taste a sugared chestnut or a chocolate; and when he declined, pleading the imminence of the dinner-hour, she murmured, 'Well, I suppose you're so used to them—living so long over here.' The allusion to the dinner-hour led Mr Dosson to express the wish that he would go round and dine with them without ceremony; they were expecting a friend—he generally settled it for them—who was coming to take them round.

'And then we are going to the circus,' Francie said, speaking for the first time.

If she had not spoken before she had done something still more to the purpose; she had removed any shade of doubt that might have lingered in the young man's spirit as to her charm of line. He was aware that his Parisian education, acting upon a natural aptitude, had opened him much—rendered him perhaps even morbidly sensitive—to impressions of this order; the society of artists, the talk of studios, the attentive study of beautiful works, the sight of a thousand forms of curious research and experiment, had produced in his mind a new sense, the exercise of which was a conscious enjoyment, and the supreme gratification of which, on several occasions, had given him as many ineffaceable memories. He had once said to his friend Waterlow: 'I don't know whether it's a confession of a very poor life, but the most important things that have happened to me in this world have been

simply half-a-dozen impressions—impressions of the eye.'
'Ah, *malheureux*, you're lost!' the painter had exclaimed,
in answer to this, and without even taking the trouble to
explain his ominous speech. Gaston Probert however
had not been frightened by it, and he continued to be
thankful for the sensitive plate that nature (with culture
added), enabled him to carry in his brain. The impression
of the eye was doubtless not everything, but it was so
much gained, so much saved, in a world in which other
treasures were apt to slip through one's fingers; and
above all it had the merit that so many things gave it and
that nothing could take it away. He had perceived in a
moment that Francie Dosson gave it; and now, seeing her
a second time, he felt that she conferred it in a degree
which made acquaintance with her one of those 'important' facts of which he had spoken to Charles Waterlow.
It was in the case of such an accident as this that he felt
the value of his Parisian education—his modern sense.

It was therefore not directly the prospect of the circus
that induced him to accept Mr Dosson's invitation; nor
was it even the charm exerted by the girl's appearing, in
the few words she uttered, to appeal to him for herself.
It was his feeling that on the edge of the glittering ring
her type would form his entertainment and that if he
knew it was rare she herself did not. He liked to be conscious, but he liked others not to be. It seemed to him at
this moment, after he had told Mr Dosson he should be
delighted to spend the evening with them, that he was
indeed trying hard to discover how it would feel to be an

American; he had jumped on the ship, he was pitching away to the west. He had led his sister, Mme de Brécourt, to expect that he would dine with her (she was having a little party), and if she could see the people to whom, without a scruple, with a quick sense of refreshment and freedom, he now sacrificed her! He knew who was coming to his sister's, in the Place Beauvau: Mme d'Outreville and M. de Grospré, old M. Courageau, Mme de Brives, Lord and Lady Trantum, Mlle de Saintonge; but he was fascinated by the idea of the contrast between what he preferred and what he gave up. His life had long been wanting—painfully wanting—in the element of contrast, and here was a chance to bring it in. He seemed to see it come in powerfully with Mr Flack, after Miss Dosson had proposed that they should walk off without their initiator. Her father did not favour this suggestion; he said, 'We want a double good dinner to-day and Mr Flack has got to order it.' Upon this Delia had asked the visitor if *he* couldn't order—a Frenchman like him; and Francie had interrupted, before he could answer the question— 'Well, *are* you a Frenchman? that's just the point, isn't it?' Gaston Probert replied that he had no wish but to be of *her* nationality, and the elder sister asked him if he knew many Americans in Paris. He was obliged to confess that he did not, but he hastened to add that he was eager to go on, now that he had made such a charming beginning.

'Oh, we ain't anything—if you mean that,' said the young lady. 'If you go on you'll go on beyond us.'

'We ain't anything here, my dear, but we are a good deal at home,' Mr Dosson remarked, smiling.

'I think we are very nice anywhere!' Francie exclaimed; upon which Gaston Probert declared that they were as delightful as possible. It was in these amenities that George Flack found them engaged; but there was none the less a certain eagerness in his greeting of the other guest, as if he had it in mind to ask him how soon he could give him half an hour. I hasten to add that, with the turn the occasion presently took, the correspondent of the *Reverberator* renounced the effort to put Mr Probert down. They all went out together, and the professional impulse, usually so irresistible in George Flack's mind, suffered a modification. He wanted to put his fellow-visitor down, but in a more human, a more passionate sense. Probert talked very little to Francie, but though Mr Flack did not know that on a first occasion he would have thought that violent, even rather gross, he knew it was for Francie, and Francie alone, that the fifth member of the party was there. He said to himself suddenly and in perfect sincerity that it was a mean class any way, the people for whom their own country was not good enough. He did not go so far however when they were seated at the admirable establishment of M. Durand, in the Place de la Madeleine, as to order a bad dinner to spite his competitor; nor did he, to spoil this gentleman's amusement, take uncomfortable seats at the pretty circus in the Champs Elysées to which, at half-past eight o'clock, the company was conveyed (it was a drive of but five minutes) in a couple of cabs. The occasion therefore was superficially smooth, and he could see that the sense of being disagreeable to an American newspaper-man was not needed to make his nondescript rival enjoy it. He hated his accent, he hated his laugh, and he hated above all the lamblike way their companions accepted him. Mr Flack was quite acute enough to make an important observation: he cherished it and promised himself to bring it to the notice of his gullible friends. Gaston Probert professed a great desire to be of service to the young ladies—to do something which would help them to be happy in Paris; but he gave no hint of an intention to do that which would contribute most to such a result—bring them in contact with the other members, and above all with the female members, of his family. George Flack knew nothing about the matter, but he required for purposes of argument that Mr Probert's family should have female members, and it was lucky for him that his assumption was just. He thought he foresaw the effect with which he should impress it upon Francie and Delia (but above all upon Delia, who would then herself impress it upon Francie), that it would be time for their French friend to talk when he had brought his mother round. *But he never would*—they might bet their pile on that! He never did, in the sequel, in fact—having, poor young man, no mother to bring. Moreover he was mum (as Delia phrased it to herself) about Mme de Brécourt and Mme de Cliché: such, Miss Dosson learned from Charles Waterlow, were the names of his two sisters who had houses in Paris—gathering at the same time the information that one of these ladies was a *marquise* and the other a *comtesse*. She was less exasperated by their non-appearance than Mr Flack had hoped, and it did not prevent an excursion to dine at Saint-Germain, a week after the evening spent at the circus, which included both of the new admirers. It also as a matter of course included Mr Flack, for though the party had been proposed in the first instance by Charles Waterlow, who wished to multiply opportunities for studying his future sitter, Mr Dosson had characteristically constituted himself host and administrator, with the young journalist as his deputy. He liked to invite people and to pay for them, and he disliked to be invited and paid for. He was never inwardly content, on any occasion, unless a great deal of money was spent, and he could be sure enough of the magnitude of the sum only when he himself spent it. He was too simple for conceit or for pride of purse, but he always felt that any arrangements were a little shabby as to which the expenses had not been referred to him. He never told anyone how he met them. Moreover Delia had told him that if they should go to Saint-Germain as guests of the artist and his friend Mr Flack would not be of the company: she was sure those gentlemen would not invite him. In fact she was too acute, for though he liked him little, Charles Waterlow would on this occasion have made a point of expressing by a hospitable attitude his sense of obligation to a man who had brought him such a subject. Delia's hint however was all-sufficient for her father; he would have thought it a gross breach of friendly loyalty to take part in a festival not graced by Mr Flack's presence. His idea of loyalty was that he should scarcely smoke a cigar unless his friend was there to take another, and he felt rather mean if he went round alone to get shaved. As regards Saint-Germain, he took over the project and George Flack telegraphed for a table on the terrace at the Pavillon Henri Quatre. Mr Dosson had by this time learned to trust the European manager of the *Reverberator* to spend his money almost as he himself would.

IV

DELIA had broken out the evening they took Mr Probert to the circus; she had apostrophised Francie as they each sat in a red-damask chair after ascending to their apartments. They had bade their companions farewell at the door of the hotel and the two gentlemen had walked off in different directions. But up stairs they had instinctively not separated; they dropped into the first place and sat looking at each other and at the highly-decorated lamps that burned, night after night, in their empty saloon. 'Well, I want to know when you're going to stop,' Delia said to her sister, speaking as if this remark were a continuation, which it was not, of something they had lately been saying.

'Stop what?' asked Francie, reaching forward for a *marron*.

'Stop carrying on the way you do—with Mr Flack.'

Francie stared, while she consumed her *marron*; then she replied, in her little flat, patient voice, 'Why, Delia Dosson, how can you be so foolish?'

'Father, I wish you'd speak to her. Francie, I ain't foolish.'

'What do you want me to say to her?' Mr Dosson inquired. 'I guess I've said about all I know.'

'Well, that's in fun; I want you to speak to her in earnest.'

'I guess there's no one in earnest but you,' Francie remarked. 'These are not so good as the last.'

'No, and there won't be if you don't look out. There's something you can do if you'll just keep quiet. If you can't tell difference of style, well, I can.'

'What's the difference of style?' asked Mr Dosson. But before this question could be answered Francie protested against the charge of carrying on. Quiet? Wasn't she as quiet as a stopped clock? Delia replied that a girl was not quiet so long as she didn't keep others so; and she wanted to know what her sister proposed to do about Mr Flack. 'Why don't you take him and let Francie take the other?' Mr Dosson continued.

'That's just what I'm after—to make her take the other,' said his elder daughter.

'Take him—how do you mean?' Francie inquired.

'Oh, you know how.'

'Yes, I guess you know how!' Mr Dosson laughed,

with an absence of prejudice which might have been thought deplorable in a parent.

'Do you want to stay in Europe or not? that's what I want to know,' Delia declared to her sister. 'If you want to go bang home you're taking the right way to do it.'

'What has that got to do with it?' asked Mr Dosson.

'Should you like so much to reside at that place—where is it?—where his paper is published? That's where you'll have to pull up, sooner or later,' Delia pursued.

'Do you want to stay in Europe, father?' Francie said, with her small sweet weariness.

'It depends on what you mean by staying. I want to go home some time.'

'Well, then, you've got to go without Mr Probert,' Delia remarked with decision. 'If you think he wants to live over there——'

'Why, Delia, he wants dreadfully to go—he told me so himself,' Francie argued, with passionless pauses.

'Yes, and when he gets there he'll want to come back. I thought you were so much interested in Paris.'

'My poor child, I *am* interested!' smiled Francie. 'Ain't I interested, father?'

'Well, I don't know how you could act differently to show it.'

'Well, I do then,' said Delia. 'And if you don't make Mr Flack understand I will.'

'Oh, I guess he understands—he's so bright,' Francie returned.

'Yes, I guess he does—he *is* bright,' said Mr Dosson. 'Good-night, chickens,' he added; and wandered off to a couch of untroubled repose.

His daughters sat up half-an-hour later, but not by the wish of the younger girl. She was always passive however, always docile when Delia was, as she said, on the war-path, and though she had none of her sister's insistence she was very courageous in suffering. She thought Delia whipped her up too much, but there was that in her which would have prevented her from ever running away. She could smile and smile for an hour without irritation, making even pacific answers, though all the while her companion's grossness hurt something delicate that was in her. She knew that Delia loved her—not loving herself meanwhile a bit—as no one else in the world probably ever would; and there was something droll in such plans for her—plans of ambition which could only involve a loss. The real answer to anything, to everything Delia might say in her moods of prefigurement was —'Oh, if you want to make out that people are thinking of me or that they ever will, you ought to remember that no one can possibly think of me half as much as you do. Therefore if there is to be any comfort for either of us we had both much better just go on as we are.' She did not however, on this occasion, meet her sister with this syllogism, because there happened to be a certain fascination in the way Delia set forth the great truth that the star of matrimony, for the American girl, was now shining in the east—in England and France and Italy. They had only to look round anywhere to see it: what did they hear of every day in the week but of the engagement of one of their own compeers to some count or some lord? Delia insisted on the fact that it was in that vast, vague section of the globe to which she never alluded save as 'over here' that the American girl was now called upon to play, under providence, her part. When Francie remarked that Mr Probert was not a count nor a lord her sister rejoined that she didn't care whether he was or not. To this Francie replied that she herself didn't care but that Delia ought to, to be consistent.

'Well, he's a prince compared with Mr Flack,' Delia declared.

'He hasn't the same ability; not half.'

'He has the ability to have three sisters who are just the sort of people I want you to know.'

'What good will they do me?' Francie asked. 'They'll hate me. Before they could turn round I should do something—in perfect innocence—that they would think monstrous.'

'Well, what would that matter if *he* liked you?'

'Oh, but he wouldn't then! He would hate me too.'

'Then all you've got to do is not to do it,' Delia said.

'Oh, but I should—every time,' her sister went on.

Delia looked at her a moment. 'What *are* you talking about?'

'Yes, what am I? It's disgusting!' And Francie sprang up.

'I'm sorry you have such thoughts,' said Delia, sententiously.

'It's disgusting to talk about a gentleman—and his sisters and his society and everything else—before he has scarcely looked at you.'

'It's disgusting if he isn't just dying; but it isn't if he is.'

'Well, I'll make him skip!' Francie went on.

'Oh, you're worse than father!' her sister cried, giving her a push as they went to bed.

They reached Saint-Germain with their companions nearly an hour before the time that had been fixed for dinner; the purpose of this being to enable them to enjoy with what remained of daylight a stroll on the celebrated terrace and a study of the magnificent view. The evening was splendid and the atmosphere favourable to this entertainment; the grass was vivid on the broad walk beside the parapet, the park and forest were fresh and leafy and the prettiest golden light hung over the curving Seine and the far-spreading city. The hill which forms the terrace stretched down among the vineyards, with the poles delicate yet in their bareness, to the river, and the prospect was spotted here and there with the red legs of the little sauntering soldiers of the garrison. How it came, after Delia's warning in regard to her carrying on (especially as she had not failed to feel the force of her sister's wisdom), Francie could not have told herself: certain it is that before ten minutes had elapsed she perceived, first, that the evening would not pass without Mr Flack's taking in some way, and for a certain time, peculiar possession of her; and then that he was already doing so, that he had drawn her away from the others, who were stopping behind them to exclaim upon the view, that he made her walk faster, and that he ended by interposing such a distance that she was practically alone with him. This was what he wanted, but it was not all; she felt that he wanted a great many other things. The large perspective of the terrace stretched away before them (Mr Probert had said it was in the grand style), and he was determined to make her walk to the end. She felt sorry for his determinations; they were an idle exercise of a force intrinsically fine, and she wanted to protest, to let him know that it was really a waste of his great cleverness to count upon her. She was not to be counted on; she was a vague, soft, negative being who had never decided anything and never would, who had not even the merit of coquetry and who only asked to be let alone. She made him stop at last, telling him, while she leaned against the parapet, that he walked too fast; and she looked back at their companions, whom she expected to see, under pressure from Delia, following at the highest speed. But they were not following; they still stood there, only looking, attentively enough, at the absent members of the party. Delia would wave her parasol, beckon her back, send Mr Waterlow to bring her; Francie looked from one moment to another for some such manifestation as that. But no manifestation came; none at least but the odd spectacle, presently, of the group turning round and, evidently under Delia's direction, retracing its steps. Francie guessed in a moment what was meant by that; it was the most definite signal her sister could have given. It made her feel that Delia counted on her, but to such a different end, just as poor Mr Flack did, just as Delia wished to persuade her that Mr Probert did. The girl gave a sigh, looking up at her companion with troubled eyes, at the idea of being made the object of converging policies. Such a thankless, bored, evasive little object as she felt herself! What Delia had said in turning away was—'Yes, I am watching you, and I depend upon you to finish him up. Stay there with him —go off with him (I'll give you half an hour if necessary), only settle him once for all. It is very kind of me to give you this chance; and in return for it I expect you to be able to tell me this evening that he has got his answer. Shut him up!'

Francie did not in the least dislike Mr Flack. Interested as I am in presenting her favourably to the reader I am yet obliged as a veracious historian to admit that he seemed to her decidedly a brilliant being. In many a girl the sort of appreciation she had of him might easily have been converted by peremptory treatment from outside into something more exalted. I do not misrepresent the perversity of women in saying that our young lady might at this moment have replied to her sister with: 'No, I was not in love with him, but somehow since you are so very prohibitive I foresee that I shall be if he asks me.' It is doubtless difficult to say more for Francie's simplicity of character than that she felt no need of encouraging Mr Flack in order to prove to herself that she was not bullied. She didn't care whether she were bullied or not; and she was perfectly capable of letting her sister believe that she had carried mildness to the point of giving up a man she had a secret sentiment for in order to oblige that large-brained young lady. She was not clear herself as to whether it might not be so; her pride, what she had of it, lay in an undistributed, inert form quite at the bottom of her heart, and she had never yet invented any consoling theory to cover her want of a high spirit. She felt, as she looked up at Mr Flack, that she didn't care even if he should think that she sacrificed him to a childish sub-servience. His bright eyes were hard, as if he could almost guess how cynical she was, and she turned her own again towards her retreating companions. 'They are going to dinner; we oughtn't to be dawdling here,' she said.

'Well, if they are going to dinner they'll have to eat the napkins. I ordered it and I know when it will be ready,' George Flack replied. 'Besides, they are not going to dinner, they are going to walk in the park. Don't you worry, we sha'n't lose them. I wish we could!' the young man added, smiling.

'You wish we could?'

'I should like to feel that you were under my particular protection.'

'Well, I don't know what the dangers are,' said Francie, setting herself in motion again. She went after the others, but at the end of a few steps he stopped her again.

'You won't have confidence. I wish you would believe what I tell you.'

'You haven't told me anything.' And she turned her

back to him, looking away at the splendid view. 'I admire the scenery,' she added in a moment.

'Oh, bother the scenery! I want to tell you something about myself, if I could flatter myself that you would take any interest in it.' He had thrust his cane, waist-high, into the low wall of the terrace, and he leaned against it, screwing the point gently round with both hands.

'I'll take an interest if I can understand,' said Francie.

'You can understand easy enough, if you'll try. I've got some news from America to-day that has pleased me very much. The *Reverberator* has taken a jump.'

This was not what Francie had expected, but it was better. 'Taken a jump?' she repeated.

'It has gone straight up. It's in the second hundred thousand.'

'Hundred thousand dollars?' said Francie.

'No, Miss Francie, copies. That's the circulation. But the dollars are footing up, too.'

'And do they all come to you?'

'Precious few of them! I wish they did; it's a pleasant property.'

'Then it isn't yours?' she asked, turning round to him. It was an impulse of sympathy that made her look at him now, for she already knew how much he had the success of his newspaper at heart. He had once told her he loved the *Reverberator* as he had loved his first jack-knife.

'Mine? You don't mean to say you suppose I own it!' George Flack exclaimed. The light projected upon her innocence by these words was so strong that the girl blushed, and he went on more tenderly—'It's a pretty sight, the way you and your sister take that sort of thing for granted. Do you think property grows on you, like a moustache? Well, it seems as if it had, on your father. If I owned the *Reverberator* I shouldn't be stumping round here; I'd give my attention to another branch of the business. That is I would give my attention to all, but I wouldn't go round with the cart. But I'm going to get hold of it, and I want you to help me,' the young man went on; 'that's just what I wanted to speak to you about. It's a big thing already and I mean to make it bigger: the most universal society-paper the world has seen. That's where the future lies, and the man who sees it first is the man who'll make his pile. It's a field for enlightened enterprise that hasn't yet begun to be worked.' He continued, glowing, almost suddenly, with his idea, and one of his eyes half closed itself knowingly, in a way that was habitual with him when he talked consecutively. The effect of this would have been droll to a listener, the note of the prospectus mingling with the accent of passion. But it was not droll to Francie; she only thought it, or supposed it, a proof of the way Mr Flack saw everything in its largest relations. 'There are ten thousand things to do that haven't been done, and I am going to do them. The society news of every quarter of the globe, furnished by the prominent members themselves (oh, *they* can be fixed—you'll see!) from day to day and from hour to hour and served up at every breakfast-table in the

United States—that's what the American people want
and that's what the American people are going to have.
I wouldn't say it to every one, but I don't mind telling
you, that I consider I have about as fine a sense as any one
of what's going to be required in future over there. I'm
going for the secrets, the *chronique intime,* as they say
here; what the people want is just what isn't told, and I'm
going to tell it. Oh, they're bound to have the plums!
That's about played out, any way, the idea of sticking up
a sign of "private" and thinking you can keep the place to
yourself. You can't do it—you can't keep out the light of
the Press. Now what I am going to do is to set up the
biggest lamp yet made and to make it shine all over the
place. We'll see who's private then! I'll make them crowd
in themselves with the information, and as I tell you, Miss
Francie, it's a job in which you can give me a lovely
push.'

'Well, I don't see how,' said Francie, candidly. 'I
haven't got any secrets.' She spoke gaily, because she was
relieved; she thought she had in reality a glimpse of what
he wanted of her. It was something better than she had
feared. Since he didn't own the great newspaper (her conception of such matters was of the dimmest), he desired
to possess himself of it, and she sufficiently comprehended that money was needed for that. She further
seemed to perceive that he presented himself to her as
moneyless and that this brought them round by a vague
but comfortable transition to a pleasant consciousness
that her father was not. The remaining induction, silently

made, was quick and happy: she should acquit herself by asking her father for the sum required and just passing it over to Mr Flack. The greatness of his enterprise and the magnitude of his conceptions appeared to over-shadow her as they stood there. This was a delightful simplification and it did not for a moment strike her as positively unnatural that her companion should have a delicacy about appealing to Mr Dosson directly for pecuniary aid, though indeed she was capable of thinking that odd if she had meditated upon it. There was nothing simpler to Francie than the idea of putting her hand into her father's pocket, and she felt that even Delia would be glad to satisfy the young man by this casual gesture. I must add unfortunately that her alarm came back to her from the way in which he replied: 'Do you mean to say you don't know, after all I've done?'

'I am sure I don't know what you've done.'

'Haven't I tried—all I know—to make you like me?'

'Oh dear, I do like you!' cried Francie; 'but how will that help you?'

'It will help me if you will understand that I love you.'

'Well, I won't understand!' replied the girl, walking off.

He followed her; they went on together in silence and then he said—'Do you mean to say you haven't found that out?'

'Oh, I don't find things out—I ain't an editor!' Francie laughed.

'You draw me out and then you jibe at me,' Mr Flack remarked.

'I didn't draw you out. Couldn't you see me just straining to get away?'

'Don't you sympathise with my ideas?'

'Of course I do, Mr Flack; I think they're splendid,' said Francie, who did not in the least understand them.

'Well, then, why won't you work with me? Your affection, your brightness, your faith would be everything to me.'

'I'm very sorry—but I can't—I can't,' the girl declared.

'You could if you would, quick enough.'

'Well, then, I won't!' And as soon as these words were spoken, as if to mitigate something of their asperity, Francie paused a moment and said: 'You must remember that I never said I would—nor anything like it. I thought you just wanted me to speak to my father.'

'Of course I supposed you would do that.'

'I mean about your paper.'

'About my paper?'

'So as he could give you the money—to do what you want.'

'Lord, you're too sweet!' George Flack exclaimed, staring. 'Do you suppose I would ever touch a cent of your father's money?'—a speech not so hypocritical as it may sound, inasmuch as the young man, who had his own refinements, had never been guilty, and proposed to himself never to be, of the plainness of twitching the purse-strings of his potential father-in-law with his own hand. He had talked to Mr Dosson by the hour about the interviewing business, but he had never dreamed that this amiable man would give him money as an interesting struggler. The only character in which he could expect it would be that of Francie's husband, and then it would come to Francie—not to him. This reasoning did not diminish his desire to assume such a character, and his love of his profession and his appreciation of the girl at his side ached together in his breast with the same disappointment. She saw that her words had touched him like a lash; they made him blush red for a moment. This caused her own colour to rise—she could scarcely have said why—and she hurried along again. He kept close to her; he argued with her; he besought her to think it over, assured her he was the best fellow in the world. To this she replied that if he didn't leave her alone she would cry—and how would he like that, to bring her back in such a state to the others? He said, 'Damn the others!' but that did not help his case, and at last he broke out: 'Will you just tell me this, then—is it because you've promised Miss Delia?' Francie answered that she had not promised Miss Delia anything, and her companion went on: 'Of course I know what she has got in her head: she wants to get you into the high set—the *grand monde*, as they call it here; but I didn't suppose you'd let her fix your life for you. You were very different before *he* turned up.'

'She never fixed anything for me. I haven't got any life and I don't want to have,' said Francie. 'And I don't know who you are talking about, either!'

'The man without a country. He'll pass you in—that's what your sister wants.'

'You oughtn't to abuse him, because it was you that presented him,' the girl rejoined.

'I never presented him! I'd like to kick him.'

'We should never have seen him if it hadn't been for you.'

'That's a fact, but it doesn't make me love him any the better. He's the poorest kind there is.'

'I don't care anything about his kind.'

'That's a pity, if you're going to marry him. How could I know that when I took you up there?'

'Good-bye, Mr Flack,' said Francie, trying to gain ground from him.

This attempt was of course vain, and after a moment he resumed: 'Will you keep me as a friend?'

'Why, Mr Flack, of course I will!' cried Francie.

'All right,' he replied; and they presently rejoined their companions.

V

GASTON PROBERT made his plan, imparting it to no one but his friend Waterlow, whose help indeed he needed to carry it out. These confidences cost him something, for the clever young painter found his predicament amusing and made no scruple of showing it. Probert was too much in love however to be discountenanced by sarcasm. This fact is the more noteworthy as he knew that

Waterlow scoffed at him for a purpose—had a theory that that kind of treatment would be salutary. The French taste was in Waterlow's 'manner', but it had not yet coloured his view of the relations of a young man of spirit with parents and pastors. He was Gallic to the tip of his finest brush, but the humour of his early American education could not fail to obtrude itself in discussion with a friend in whose life the principle of authority played so large a part. He accused Probert of being afraid of his sisters, which was a crude way (and he knew it) of alluding to the rigidity of the conception of the family among people who had adopted and had even to Waterlow's sense, as the phrase is, improved upon the usages of France. That did injustice (and this the artist also knew) to the delicate nature of the bond which united the different members of the house of Probert, who were each for all and all for each. Family feeling among them was not a tyranny but a religion, and in regard to Mesdames de Brécourt, de Cliché, and de Douves what Gaston was most afraid of was seeming to them not to love them. None the less Charles Waterlow, who thought he had charming parts, held that the best way had not been taken to make a man of him, and the spirit in which the painter sometimes endeavoured to repair this mishap was altogether benevolent though the form was frequently rough. Waterlow combined in an odd manner many of the forms of the Parisian studio with the moral and social ideas of Brooklyn, Long Island, where his first seeds had been implanted.

Gaston Probert desired nothing better than to be a man; what bothered him (and it is perhaps a proof that his instinct was gravely at fault) was a certain vagueness as to the constituents of this personage. He should be made more nearly, as it seemed to him, a brute were he to sacrifice in such an effort the decencies and pieties—holy things all of them—in which he had been reared. It was very well for Waterlow to say that to be a genuine man it was necessary to be a little of a brute; his friend was willing, in theory, to assent even to that. The difficulty was in application, in practice—as to which the painter declared that all that would be simple enough if it only didn't take so much account of the marchioness, the countess and—what was the other one?—the duchess. These young amenities were exchanged between the pair (while Gaston explained, almost as eagerly as if he were scoring a point, that the other one was only a *baronne*) during that brief journey to Spain of which mention has already been made, during the later weeks of the summer, after their return (the young men spent a fortnight together on the coast of Brittany), and above all during the autumn, when they were settled in Paris for the winter, when Mr Dosson had reappeared, according to the engagement with his daughters, when the sittings for the portrait had multiplied (the painter was unscrupulous as to the number he demanded), and the work itself, born under a happy star, took on more and more the aspect of a masterpiece. It was at Grenada that Gaston really broke out; there, one balmy night, he communicated to his companion that he would marry Francina Dosson or would never marry any one. The declaration was the more striking as it came after an interval; many days had elapsed since their separation from the young lady and many new and beautiful objects had engaged their attention. It appeared that poor Probert had been thinking of her all the while, and he let his friend know that it was that dinner at Saint-Germain that had finished him. What she had been there Waterlow himself had seen: he would not controvert the proposition that she had been irresistible.

In November, in Paris (it was months and weeks before the artist began to please himself), the enamoured youth came very often to the Avenue de Villiers, toward the end of a sitting; and until it was finished, not to disturb the lovely model, he cultivated conversation with the elder sister: Gaston Probert was capable of that. Delia was always there of course, but Mr Dosson had not once turned up and the newspaper-man happily appeared to have taken himself off. The new aspirant learned in fact from Miss Dosson that a crisis in the affairs of his journal had recalled him to the seat of that publication. When the young ladies had gone (and when he did not go with them—he accompanied them not rarely), the visitor was almost lyrical in his appreciation of his friend's work; he had no jealousy of the insight which enabled him to reconstitute the girl on canvas with that perfection. He knew that Waterlow painted her too well to be in love with her and that if he himself could have attacked her in that fashion he would not have wanted to marry her. She bloomed there, on the easel, as brightly as in life, and the artist had caught the sweet essence of her beauty. It was exactly the way in which her lover would have chosen that she should be represented, and yet it had required a perfectly independent hand. Gaston Probert mused on this mystery and somehow felt proud of the picture and responsible for it, though it was as little his property, as yet, as the young lady herself.

When, in December, he told Waterlow of his plan of campaign the latter said, 'I will do anything in the world you like—anything you think will help you—but it passes me, my dear fellow, why in the world you don't go to them and say, "I've seen a girl who is as good as cake and pretty as fire, she exactly suits me, I've taken time to think of it and I know what I want: therefore I propose to make her my wife. If you happen to like her so much the better; if you don't be so good as to keep it to yourselves." That is much the most excellent way. Why, gracious heaven, all these mysteries and machinations?'

'Oh, you don't understand, you don't understand!' sighed Gaston Probert, with many wrinkles on his brow. 'One can't break with one's traditions in an hour, especially when there is so much in them that one likes. I shall not love her more if they like her, but I shall love *them* more, and I care about that. You talk as a man who has nothing to consider. I have everything to consider— and I am glad I have. My pleasure in marrying her will be double if my father and my sisters accept her, and

I shall greatly enjoy working out the business of bringing them round.'

There were moments when Charles Waterlow resented the very terminology of his friend; he hated to hear a man talk about the woman he loved being 'accepted'. If one accepted her one's self or, rather, were accepted by her, that ended the matter, and the effort to bring round those who gave her the cold shoulder was scarcely consistent with self-respect. Probert explained that of course he knew his relatives would only have to know Francina to like her, to delight in her; but that to know her they would first have to make her acquaintance. This was the delicate point, for social commerce with such people as Mr Dosson and Delia was not in the least in their usual line and it was impossible to disconnect the poor girl from her appendages. Therefore the whole question must be approached by an oblique movement; it would never do to march straight up to it. The wedge should have a narrow end and Gaston was ready to declare that he had found it. His sister Susan was another name for it; he would break her in first and she would help him to break in the others. She was his favourite relation, his intimate friend—the most modern, the most Parisian and inflammable member of the family. She was not reasonable but she was perceptive; she had imagination and humour and was capable of generosity and enthusiasm and even of infatuation. She had had her own infatuations and ought to allow for those of others. She would not like the Dossons superficially any better than his father or than Margaret or Jane (he called these ladies by their English names, but for themselves, their husbands, their friends and each other they were Suzanne, Marguerite and Jeanne); but there was a considerable chance that he might induce her to take his point of view. She was as fond of beauty and of the arts as he was; this was one of their bonds of union. She appreciated highly Charles Waterlow's talent and there had been a good deal of talk about his painting her portrait. It is true her husband viewed the project with so much colder an eye that it had not been carried out.

According to Gaston's plan she was to come to the Avenue de Villiers to see what the artist had done for Miss Francie; her brother was to have stimulated her curiosity by his rhapsodies, in advance, rhapsodies bearing wholly upon the work itself, the example of Waterlow's powers, and not upon the young lady, whom he was not to let her know at first that he had so much as seen. Just at the last, just before her visit, he was to tell her that he had met the girl (at the studio), and that she was as remarkable in her way as the picture. Seeing the picture and hearing this, Mme de Brécourt, as a disinterested lover of charming impressions, would express a desire also to enjoy a sight of so rare a creature; upon which Waterlow was to say that that would be easy if she would come in some day when Miss Francie was sitting. He would give her two or three dates and Gaston would see that she didn't let the opportunity pass. She would return alone (this time he wouldn't go with her), and she would be as much struck as he hoped. Everything depended on that, but it couldn't fail. The girl would have to captivate her, but the girl could be trusted, especially if she didn't know who the demonstrative French lady was, with her fine plain face, her hair so flaxen as to be nearly white, her vividly red lips and protuberant, light-coloured eyes. Waterlow was to do no introducing and to reveal the visitor's identity only after she had gone. This was a charge he grumbled at; he called the whole business an odious comedy, but his friend knew that if he undertook it he would acquit himself honourably. After Mme de Brécourt had been captivated (the question of whether Francie would be so received in advance no consideration), her brother would throw off the mask and convince her that she must now work with him. Another meeting would be arranged for her with the girl (in which each would appear in her proper character), and in short the plot would thicken.

Gaston Probert's forecast of his difficulties revealed a considerable faculty for analysis, but that was not rare enough in the French composition of things to make his friend stare. He brought Suzanne de Brécourt, she was enchanted with the portrait of the little American, and the rest of the drama began to follow in its order. Mme de Brécourt raved, to Waterlow's face (she had no opinions behind people's backs), about his mastery of his craft; she could say flattering things to a man with an assurance altogether her own. She was the reverse of egotistic and never spoke of herself; her success in life sprang from a much cleverer selection of her pronouns. Waterlow, who liked her and wanted to paint her ugliness (it was so charming, as he would make it), had two opinions about her—one of which was that she knew a hundred times less than she thought (and even than her brother thought), of what she talked about; and the other that she was after all not such a humbug as she seemed. She passed in her family for a rank radical, a bold Bohemian; she picked up expressions out of newspapers, but her hands and feet were celebrated, and her behaviour was not. That of her sisters, as well, had never been effectively exposed.

'But she must be charming, your young lady,' she said to Gaston, while she turned her head this way and that as she stood before Francie's image. 'She looks like a piece of sculpture—or something cast in silver—of the time of Francis the First; something of Jean Goujon or Germain Pilon.' The young men exchanged a glance, for this happened to be a capital comparison, and Gaston replied, in a detached way, that she was well worth seeing.

He went in to have a cup of tea with his sister on the day he knew she would have paid her second visit to the studio, and the first words she greeted him with were—'But she is admirable—*votre petite*—admirable, admirable!' There was a lady calling in the Place Beauvau at the moment—old Mme d'Outreville, and she naturally asked who was the object of such enthusiasm. Gaston suffered Susan to answer this question; he wanted to hear what she would say. She described the girl almost as well as he would have done, from the point of view of the plastic, with a hundred technical and critical terms, and the old lady listened in silence, solemnly, rather coldly, as if she thought such talk a good deal of a *galimatias*: she belonged to the old-fashioned school and held that a young lady was sufficiently catalogued when it was said that she had a dazzling complexion or the finest eyes in the world.

'*Qu'est-ce que c'est que cette merveille?*' she inquired; to which Mme de Brécourt replied that it was a little American whom her brother had dug up. 'And what do you propose to do with her, may one ask?' Mme d'Outreville demanded, looking at Gaston Probert with an eye which seemed to read his secret, so that for half a minute he was on the point of breaking out: 'I propose to marry her—there!' But he contained himself, only mentioning for the present that he aspired to ascertain to what uses she was adapted; meanwhile, he added, he expected to look at her a good deal, in the measure in which she would allow him. 'Ah, that may take you far!' the old lady exclaimed, as she got up to go; and Gaston glanced at his sister, to see if this idea struck her too. But she appeared almost provokingly exempt from alarm; if she had been suspicious it would have been easier to make his confession. When he came back from accompanying Mme d'Outreville to her carriage he asked her if the girl at the studio had known who she was and if she had been frightened. Mme de Brécourt stared; she evidently thought that kind of sensibility implied an initiation which a little American, accidently encountered, could not possibly have. 'Why should she be frightened? She wouldn't be even if she had known who I was; much less therefore when I was nothing for her.'

'Oh, you were not nothing for her!' Gaston declared; and when his sister rejoined that he was too amiable he brought out his revelation. He had seen the young lady more often than he had told her; he had particularly wished that *she* should see her. Now he wanted his father and Jane and Margaret to do the same, and above all he wanted them to like her, even as she, Susan, liked her. He was delighted that she had been captivated—he had been captivated himself. Mme de Brécourt protested that she had reserved her independence of judgment, and he answered that if she had thought Miss Dosson repulsive she might have expressed it in another way. When she inquired what he was talking about and what he wanted them all to do with her, he said: 'I want you to treat her kindly, tenderly, for such as you see her I am thinking of making her my wife.'

'Mercy on us—you haven't asked her?' cried Mme de Brécourt.

'No, but I have asked her sister what she would say, and she tells me there would be no difficulty.'

'Her sister?—the little woman with the big head?'

'Her head is rather out of drawing, but it isn't a part of the affair. She is very inoffensive and she would be devoted to me.'

'For heaven's sake then keep quiet. She is as common as a dressmaker's bill.'

'Not when you know her. Besides, that has nothing to do with Francie. You couldn't find words enough a moment ago to say that Francie is exquisite, and now you will be so good as to stick to that. Come, be intelligent!'

'Do you call her by her little name, like that?' Mme de Brécourt asked, giving him another cup of tea.

'Only to you. She is perfectly simple. It is impossible to imagine anything better. And think of the delight of having that charming object before one's eyes—always, always! It makes a different thing of the future.'

'My poor child,' said Mme de Brécourt, 'you can't pick up a wife like that—the first little American that comes along. You know I hoped you wouldn't marry at all— what a pity I think it—for a man. At any rate, if you expect us to like Miss—what's her name?—Miss Fancy, all I can say is we won't. We can't!'

'I shall marry her then without your approbation.'

'Very good. But if she deprives you of that (you have always had it, you are used to it, it's a part of your life), you will hate her at the end of a month.'

'I don't care. I shall have had my month.'

'And she—poor thing?'

'Poor thing, exactly! You will begin to pity her, and that will make you cultivate her, and that will make you find how adorable she is. Then you'll like her, then you'll love her, then you'll see how discriminating I have been, and we shall all be happy together again.'

'But how can you possibly know, with such people, what you have got hold of?'

'By having the sense of delicate things. You pretend to have it, and yet in such a case as this you try to be stupid. Give that up; you might as well first as last, for the girl's an irresistible fact and it will be better to accept her than to let her accept you.'

Gaston's sister asked him if Miss Dosson had a fortune, and he said he knew nothing about that. Her father apparently was rich, but he didn't mean to ask for a penny with her. American fortunes moreover were the last things to count upon; they had seen too many examples of that. 'Papa will never listen to that,' Mme de Brécourt replied.

'Listen to what?'

'To your not finding out—to your not asking for settlements—*comme cela se fait.*'

'Excuse me, papa will find out for himself; and he will know perfectly whether to ask or whether to leave it alone. That's the sort of thing he does know. And he also knows perfectly that I am very difficult to place.'

'To place?'

'To find a wife for. I'm neither fish nor flesh. I have no country, no career, no future; I offer nothing; I bring nothing. What position under the sun do I confer? There's a fatuity in our talking as if we could make grand terms. You and the others are well enough: *qui prend mari prend pays,* and you have names which (at least so your husbands say) are tremendously illustrious. But papa and I—I ask you!'

'As a family *nous sommes très-bien,*' said Mme de

Brécourt. 'You know what we are—it doesn't need any explanation. We are as good as anything there is and have always been thought so. You might do anything you like.'

'Well, I shall never like to marry a Frenchwoman.'

'Thank you, my dear,' Mme de Brécourt exclaimed.

'No sister of mine is really French,' returned the young man.

'No brother of mine is really mad. Marry whomever you like,' Susan went on; 'only let her be the best of her kind. Let her be a lady. Trust me, I've studied life. That's the only thing that's safe.'

'Francie is the equal of the first lady in the land.'

'With that sister—with that hat? Never—never!'

'What's the matter with her hat?'

'The sister's told a story. It was a document—it described them, it classed them. And such a dialect as they speak!'

'My dear, her English is quite as good as yours. You don't even know how bad yours is,' said Gaston Probert.

'Well, I don't say "Parus" and I never asked an Englishman to marry me. You know what our feelings are,' his companion pursued; 'our convictions, our susceptibilities. We may be wrong—we may be hollow—we may be pretentious; we may not be able to say on what it all rests; but there we are, and the fact is insurmountable. It is simply impossible for us to live with vulgar people. It's a defect, no doubt; it's an immense inconvenience, and in the days we live in it's sadly against one's interest.

But we are made like that and we must understand ourselves. It's of the very essence of our nature, and of yours exactly as much as of mine or of that of the others. Don't make a mistake about it—you'll prepare for yourself a bitter future. I know what becomes of us. We suffer, we go through tortures, we die!'

The accent of passionate prophecy was in Mme de Brécourt's voice, but her brother made her no immediate answer, only indulging restlessly in several turns about the room. At last he observed, taking up his hat: 'I shall come to an understanding with her to-morrow, and the next day, about this hour, I shall bring her to see you. Meanwhile please say nothing to any one.'

Mme de Brécourt looked at him a moment; he had his hand on the knob of the door. 'What do you mean by her father's appearing rich? That's such a vague term. What do you suppose his means to be?'

'Ah, that's a question *she* would never ask!' cried the young man, passing out.

VI

THE next morning he found himself sitting on one of the red-satin sofas beside Mr Dosson, in this gentleman's private room at the Hôtel de l'Univers et de Cheltenham. Delia and Francie had established their father in the old quarters; they expected to spend the winter in Paris but they had not taken independent apartments, for they had an idea that when you lived that way it was grand but lonely—you didn't meet people on the staircase. The temperature was now such as to deprive the good gentleman of his usual resource of sitting in the court, and he had not yet discovered an effective substitute for this recreation. Without Mr Flack, at the cafés, he felt too much like a non-consumer. But he was patient and ruminant; Gaston Probert grew to like him and tried to invent amusements for him; took him to see the great markets, the sewers and the Bank of France, and put him in the way of acquiring a beautiful pair of horses (it is perhaps not superfluous to say that this was a perfectly straight proceeding on the young man's part), which Mr Dosson, little as he resembled a sporting character, found it a welcome pastime on fine afternoons to drive, with a highly scientific hand, from a smart Américaine, in the Bois de Boulogne. There was a reading-room at the banker's, where he spent hours engaged in a manner best known to himself, and he shared the great interest, the constant topic of his daughters—the portrait that was going forward in the Avenue de Villiers. This was the subject round which the thoughts of these young ladies clustered and their activity revolved; it gave a large scope to their faculty for endless repetition, for monotonous insistence, for vague and aimless discussion. On leaving Mme de Brécourt Francie's lover had written to Delia that he desired half an hour's private conversation with her father on the morrow at half-past eleven; his impatience forbade him to wait for a more canonical hour. He asked her to be so good as to arrange that Mr Dosson should be there to receive him and to keep Francie out of the way. Delia acquitted herself to the letter.

'Well, sir, what have you got to show?' asked Francie's father, leaning far back on the sofa and moving nothing but his head, and that very little, toward his interlocutor. Probert was placed sidewise, a hand on each knee, almost facing him, on the edge of the seat.

'To show, sir—what do you mean?'

'What do you do for a living? How do you subsist?'

'Oh, comfortably enough. Of course it would be criminal in you not to satisfy yourself on that point. My income is derived from three sources. First, some property left me by my dear mother. Second, a legacy from my poor brother, who had inherited a small fortune from an old relation of ours who took a great fancy to him (he went to America to see her), and which he divided among the four of us in the will he made at the time of the war.'

'The war—what war?' asked Mr Dosson.

'Why the Franco-German——'

'Oh, *that* old war!' And Mr Dosson almost laughed. 'Well?' he softly continued.

'Then my father is so good as to make me a little allowance; and some day I shall have more—from him.'

Mr Dosson was silent a moment; then he observed, 'Why, you seem to have fixed it so you live mostly on other folks.'

'I shall never attempt to live on you, sir!' This was

spoken with some vivacity by our young man; he felt the next moment that he had said something that might provoke a retort. But his companion only rejoined, mildly, impersonally:

'Well, I guess there won't be any trouble about that. And what does my daughter say?'

'I haven't spoken to her yet.'

'Haven't spoken to her?'

'I thought it more orthodox to break ground with you first.'

'Well, when I was after Mrs Dosson I guess I spoke to her quick enough,' Francie's father said, humorously. There was an element of reproach in this and Gaston Probert was mystified, for the inquiry about his means a moment before had been in the nature of a challenge. 'How will you feel if she won't have you, after you have exposed yourself this way to me?' the old gentleman went on.

'Well, I have a sort of confidence. It may be vain, but God grant not! I think she likes me personally, but what I am afraid of is that she may consider that she knows too little about me. She has never seen my people—she doesn't know what may be before her.'

'Do you mean your family—the folks at home?' said Mr Dosson. 'Don't you believe that. Delia has moused around—*she* has found out. Delia's thorough!'

'Well, we are very simple, kindly, respectable people, as you will see in a day or two for yourself. My father and sisters will do themselves the honour to wait upon you,' the young man declared, with a temerity the sense of which made his voice tremble.

'We shall be very happy to see them, sir,' Mr Dosson returned cheerfully. 'Well now, let's see,' he added, musing sociably. 'Don't you expect to embrace any regular occupation?'

Probert looked at him, smiling. 'Have *you* anything of that sort, sir?'

'Well, you have me there!' Mr Dosson admitted, with a comprehensive sigh. 'It doesn't seem as if I required anything, I'm looked after so well. The fact is the girls support me.'

'I shall not expect Miss Francie to support me,' said Gaston Probert.

'You're prepared to enable her to live in the style to which she's accustomed?' And Mr Dosson turned a speculative eye upon him.

'Well, I don't think she will miss anything. That is, if she does she will find other things instead.'

'I presume she'll miss Delia, and even me, a little.'

'Oh, it's easy to prevent that,' said Gaston Probert.

'Well, of course we shall be on hand. Continue to reside in Paris?' Mr Dosson went on.

'I will live anywhere in the world she likes. Of course my people are here—that's a great tie. I am not without hope that it may—with time—become a reason for your daughter.'

'Oh, any reason'll do where Paris is concerned. Take some lunch?' Mr Dosson added, looking at his watch.

They rose to their feet, but before they had gone many steps (the meals of this amiable family were now served in an adjoining room), the young man stopped his companion. 'I can't tell you how kind I think it—the way you treat me, and how I am touched by your confidence. You take me just as I am, with no recommendation beyond my own word.'

'Well, Mr Probert, if we didn't like you we wouldn't smile on you. Recommendations in that case wouldn't be any good. And since we do like you there ain't any call for them either. I trust my daughters; if I didn't I'd have stayed at home. And if I trust them, and they trust you, it's the same as if *I* trusted you, ain't it?'

'I guess it is!' said Gaston, smiling.

His companion laid his hand on the door but he paused a moment. 'Now are you very sure?'

'I thought I was, but you make me nervous.'

'Because there was a gentleman here last year—I'd have put my money on *him*.'

'A gentleman—last year?'

'Mr Flack. You met him surely. A very fine man. I thought she favoured him.'

'*Seigneur Dieu!*' Gaston Probert murmured, under his breath.

Mr Dosson had opened the door; he made his companion pass into the little dining-room, where the table was spread for the noonday breakfast. 'Where are the chickens?' he inquired, disappointedly. Gaston thought at first that he missed a dish from the board, but he recognised the next moment the old man's usual designation of his daughters. These young ladies presently came in, but Francie looked away from Mr Probert. The suggestion just dropped by her father had given him a shock (the idea of the girl's 'favouring' the newspaper-man was inconceivable), but the charming way she avoided his eye convinced him that he had nothing to fear from Mr Flack.

That night (it had been an exciting day), Delia remarked to her sister that of course she could draw back: upon which Francie repeated the expression, interrogatively, not understanding it. 'You can send him a note, saying you won't,' Delia explained.

'Won't marry him?'

'Gracious, no! Won't go to see his sister. You can tell him it's her place to come to see you first.'

'Oh, I don't care,' said Francie, wearily.

Delia looked at her a moment very gravely. 'Is that the way you answered him when he asked you?'

'I'm sure I don't know. He could tell you best.'

'If you were to speak to me that way I should have said, "Oh, well, if you don't want it any more than that!"'

'Well, I wish it was you,' said Francie.

'That Mr Probert was me?'

'No; that you were the one he liked.'

'Francie Dosson, are you thinking of Mr Flack?' her sister broke out, suddenly.

'No, not much.'

'Well then, what's the matter?'

'You have ideas and opinions; you know whose place

it is and what's due and what isn't. You could meet them all.'

'Why, how can you say, when that's just what I'm trying to find out!'

'It doesn't matter any way; it will never come off,' said Francie.

'What do you mean by that?'

'He'll give me up in a few weeks. I shall do something.'

'If you say that again I shall think you do it on purpose!' Delia declared. '*Are* you thinking of George Flack?' she repeated in a moment.

'Oh, do leave him alone!' Francie replied, in one of her rare impatiences.

'Then why are you so queer?'

'Oh, I'm tired!' said Francie, turning away. And this was the simple truth; she was tired of the consideration her sister saw fit to devote to the question of Mr Probert's not having, since their return to Paris, brought his belongings to see them. She was overdone with Delia's theories on this subject, which varied from day to day, from the assertion that he was keeping his intercourse with his American friends hidden from them because they were uncompromising in their grandeur, to the doctrine that that grandeur would descend some day upon the Hôtel de l'Univers et de Cheltenham and carry Francie away in a blaze of glory. Sometimes Delia put forth the view that they ought to make certain of Gaston's omissions the ground of a challenge; at other times she opined that they ought to take no notice of them. Francie, in this connection, had no theories, no impulses of her own; and now she was all at once happy and freshly glad and in love and sceptical and frightened and indifferent. Her lover had talked to her but little about his kinsfolk, and she had noticed this circumstance the more because of a remark dropped by Charles Waterlow to the effect that he and his father were great friends: the word seemed to her odd in that application. She knew Gaston saw that gentleman, and the exalted ladies Mr Probert's daughters, very often, and she therefore took for granted that they knew he saw her. But the most he had done was to say they would come and see her like a shot if once they should believe they could trust her. She had wished to know what he meant by their trusting her, and he had explained that it would appear to them too good to be true—that she should be kind to *him*: something exactly of that sort was what they dreamed of for him. But they had dreamed before and been disappointed, and now they were on their guard. From the moment they should feel they were on solid ground they would join hands and dance round her. Francie's answer to this fanciful statement was that she didn't know what the young man was talking about, and he indulged in no attempt on that occasion to render his meaning more clear; the consequence of which was that he felt he made a poor appearance. His uneasiness had not passed away, for many things in truth were dark to him. He could not see his father fraternising with Mr Dosson, he could not see

Margaret and Jane recognising an alliance in which Delia was one of the allies. He had answered for them because that was the only thing to do; and this only just failed to be criminally reckless. What saved it was the hope he founded upon Mme de Brécourt and the sense of how well he could answer to the others for Francie. He considered that Susan had, in her first judgment of this young lady, committed herself; she had really comprehended her, and her subsequent protest when she found what was in his heart had been a retraction which he would make her in turn retract. The girl had been revealed to her, and she would come round. A simple interview with Francie would suffice for this result: he promised himself that at the end of half an hour she should be an enthusiastic convert. At the end of an hour she would believe that she herself had invented the match—had discovered the damsel. He would pack her off to the others as the author of the project; she would take it all upon herself, would represent her brother even as a little tepid. *She* would show nothing of that sort, but boast of her wisdom and energy; and she would enjoy the comedy so that she would forget she had opposed him even for a moment. Gaston Probert was a very honourable young man, but his programme involved a good many fibs.

VII

It may as well be said at once that it was eventually carried out, and that in the course of a fortnight old Mr Probert and his daughters alighted successively at the Hôtel de l'Univers et de Cheltenham. Francie's visit with her intended to Mme de Brécourt bore exactly the fruit the young man had foreseen and was followed the very next day by a call from this lady. She took Francie out with her in her carriage and kept her the whole afternoon, driving her over half Paris, chattering with her, kissing her, delighting in her, telling her they were already sisters, paying her compliments which made the girl envy her art of beautiful expression. After she had carried her home the countess rushed off to her father's, reflecting with pleasure that at that hour she should probably find her sister Marguerite there. Mme de Cliché was with the old man in fact (she had three days in the week for coming to the Cours la Reine); she sat near him in the firelight. telling him presumably her troubles; for Maxime de Cliché was not quite the pearl that they originally had supposed. Mme de Brécourt knew what Marguerite did whenever she took that little ottoman and drew it close to her father's chair: she gave way to her favourite vice, that of dolefulness, which lengthened her long face more; it was unbecoming, if she only knew it. The family was intensely united, as we know; but that did not prevent Mme de Brécourt's having a certain sympathy for

Maxime: he too was one of themselves and she asked herself what *she* would have done if she had been a well-con-
stituted man with a wife whose cheeks were like decks in
a high sea. It was the twilight hour in the winter days,
before the lamps, that especially brought her out; then
she began her plaintive, complicated stories, to which her
father listened with such angelic patience. Mme de Brécourt liked his particular room in the old house in the
Cours la Reine; it reminded her of her mother's life and
her young days and her dead brother and the feelings
connected with her first going into the world. Alphonse
and she had had an apartment, by her father's kindness,
under that familiar roof, so that she continued to pop in
and out, full of her fresh impressions of society, just as
she had done when she was a girl. She broke into her
sister's confidences now; she announced her *trouvaille*
and did battle for it bravely.

Five days later (there had been lively work in the
meantime; Gaston turned so pale at moments that she
feared it would all result in a mortal illness for him, and
Marguerite shed gallons of tears) Mr Probert went to see
the Dossons with his son. Mme de Brécourt paid them
another visit, a kind of official affair as she deemed it,
accompanied by her husband; and the Baron de Douves
and his wife, written to by Gaston, by his father and by
Margaret and Susan, came up from the country full of
tension and responsibility. M. de Douves was the person
who took the family, all round, most seriously and most
deprecated anything in the nature of crude and precipitate

action. He was a very small black gentleman, with thick eyebrows and high heels (in the country, in the mud, he wore *sabots* with straw in them), who was suspected by his friends of believing that he looked like Louis XIV. It is perhaps a proof that something of the quality of this monarch was really recognised in him that no one had ever ventured to clear up this point by a question. '*La famille c'est moi*' appeared to be his tacit formula, and he carried his umbrella (he had very bad ones), with a kind of sceptral air. Mme de Brécourt went so far as to believe that his wife, in confirmation of this, took herself in a manner for Mme de Maintenon: she had lapsed into a provincial existence as she might have harked back to the seventeenth century; the world she lived in seemed about as far away. She was the largest, heaviest member of the family, and in the Vendée she was thought majestic, in spite of old clothes, of which she was fond and which added to her look of having come down from a remote past or reverted to it. She was at bottom an excellent woman, but she wrote *roy* and *foy* like her husband, and the action of her mind was wholly restricted to questions of relationship and alliance. She had an extraordinary patience of research and tenacity of grasp of a clue, and viewed people solely in the light projected upon them by others; that is, not as good or wicked, ugly or handsome, wise or foolish, but as grandsons, nephews, uncles and aunts, brothers and sisters-in-law, cousins and second cousins. There was a certain expectation that she would leave memoirs. In Mme de Brécourt's eyes this pair were very shabby, they did not *payer de mine*—they fairly smelt of their province; 'but for the reality of the thing,' she often said to herself, 'they are worth all of us. We are diluted and they are pure, and any one with an eye would see it.' 'The thing' was the legitimist principle, the ancient faith and even, a little, the grand air.

The Marquis de Cliché did his duty with his wife, who mopped the decks, as Susan said, for the occasion, and was entertained in the red-satin drawing-room by Mr Dosson, Delia and Francie. Mr Dosson wanted to go out when he heard of the approach of Gaston's relations, and the young man had to instruct him that this wouldn't do. The apartment in question had had a various experience, but it had probably never witnessed stranger doings than these laudable social efforts. Gaston was taught to feel that his family made a great sacrifice for him, but in a very few days he said to himself that he was safe, now they knew the worst. They made the sacrifice, they definitely agreed to it, but they judged it well that he should measure the full extent of it. 'Gaston must never, never, never be allowed to forget what we have done for him': Mme de Brécourt told him that Marguerite de Cliché had expressed herself in that sense, at one of the family conclaves from which he had been absent. These high commissions sat, for several days, with great frequency, and the young man could feel that if there was help for him in discussion his case was promising. He flattered himself that he showed infinite patience and tact, and his expenditure of the latter quality in particular was in itself his only reward, for it was impossible he should tell Francie what arts he had to practise for her. He liked to think, however, that he practised them successfully; for he held that it was by such arts the civilised man is distinguished from the savage. What they cost him was made up simply in this—that his private irritation produced a kind of cheerful glow in regard to Mr Dosson and Delia, whom he could not defend nor lucidly explain nor make people like, but whom he had ended, after so many days of familiar intercourse, by liking extremely himself. The way to get on with them—it was an immense simplification—was just to love them; one could do that even if one couldn't talk with them. He succeeded in making Mme de Brécourt seize this *nuance*; she embraced the idea with her quick inflammability. 'Yes,' she said, 'we must insist on their positive, not on their negative merits: their infinite generosity, their native delicacy. Their native delicacy above all; we must work that!' And the brother and sister excited each other magnanimously to this undertaking. Sometimes, it must be added, they exchanged a glance which expressed a sudden slightly alarmed sense of the responsibility they had put on.

On the day Mr Probert called at the Hôtel de l'Univers et de Cheltenham with his son, the pair walked away together, back to the Cours la Reine, without any immediate conversation. All that was said was some words of Mr Probert's, with Gaston's rejoinder, as they crossed the Place de la Concorde.

'We should have to have them to dinner.'

The young man noted his father's conditional, as if his acceptance of the Dossons were not yet complete; but he guessed all the same that the sight of them had not made a difference for the worse: they had let the old gentleman down more easily than was to have been feared. The call had not been noisy—a confusion of sounds; which was very happy, for Mr Probert was particular in this—he could bear French noise but he could not bear American. As for English, he maintained that there was none. Mr Dosson had scarcely spoken to him and yet had remained perfectly placid, which was exactly what Gaston would have chosen. Francie's lover knew moreover (though he was a little disappointed that no charmed exclamation should have been dropped as they quitted the hotel), that her spell had worked: it was impossible the old man should not have liked her.

'Ah, do ask them, and let it be very soon,' he replied. 'They'll like it so much.'

'And whom can they meet—who can meet *them*?'

'Only the family—all of us: *au complet*. Other people we can have later.'

'All of us, *au complet*—that makes eight. And the three of them,' said Mr Probert. Then he added, 'Poor creatures!' This exclamation gave Gaston much pleasure; he passed his hand into his father's arm. It promised well; it denoted a sentiment of tenderness for the dear little Dossons, confronted with a row of fierce French critics, judged by standards that they had never even heard of. The meeting of the two parents had not made the problem of their commerce any more clear; but young Probert was reminded freshly by his father's ejaculation of that characteristic kindness which was really what he had built upon. The old gentleman, heaven knew, had prejudices, but if they were numerous, and some of them very curious, they were not rigid. He had also such nice inconsistent feelings, such irrepressible indulgences, and they would ease everything off. He was in short an old darling, and with an old darling, in the long run, one was always safe. When they reached the house in the Cours la Reine Mr Probert said: 'I think you told me you are dining out.'

'Yes, with our friends.'

' "Our friends?" *Comme vous y allez!* Come in and see me, then, on your return; but not later than half-past ten.'

From this the young man saw that he had swallowed the dose; if he had made up his mind that it wouldn't do he would have announced the circumstance without more delay. This reflection was most agreeable, for Gaston was perfectly aware of how little he himself would have enjoyed a struggle. He would have carried it through, but he could not bear to think of it, and the sense that he was spared it made him feel at peace with all the world. The dinner at the hotel became a little banquet in honour of this state of things, especially as Francie and Delia raved, as they said, about his papa.

'Well, I expected something nice, but he goes far beyond!' Delia remarked. 'That's my idea of a gentleman.'

'Ah, for that ——!' said Gaston.

'He's so sweet. I'm not a bit afraid of him,' Francie declared.

'Why should you be?'

'Well, I am of you,' the girl went on.

'Much you show it!' her lover exclaimed.

'Yes, I am,' she insisted, 'at the bottom of all.'

'Well, that's what a lady should be—of her husband.'

'Well, I don't know; I'm more afraid than that. You'll see.'

'I wish you were afraid of talking nonsense,' said Gaston Probert.

Mr Dosson made no observation whatever about their honourable visitor; he listened in genial, unprejudiced silence. It is a sign of his prospective son-in-law's perfect comprehension of him that Gaston knew this silence not to be in any degree restrictive: it did not mean that he had not been pleased. Mr Dosson had simply nothing to say; he had not, like Gaston, a sensitive plate in his brain, and the important events of his life had never been personal impressions. His mind had had absolutely no history of that sort, and Mr Probert's appearance had not produced a revolution. If the young man had asked him how he liked his father he would have said, at the most, 'Oh, I guess he's all right!' But what was more candid even than this, in Gaston's view (and it was quite touchingly so), was the attitude of the good gentleman and his daughters toward the others, Mesdames de Douves, de Brécourt and de Cliché and their husbands, who had now all filed before them. They believed that the ladies and the gentlemen alike had covered them with endearments, were candidly, gushingly glad to make their acquaintance. They had not in the least seen what was manner, the minimum of decent profession, and what the subtle resignation of old races who have known a long historical discipline and have conventional forms for their feelings —forms resembling singularly little the feelings themselves. Francie took people at their word when they told her that the whole *manière d'être* of her family inspired them with an irresistible sympathy: that was a speech of which Mme de Cliché had been capable, speaking as if for all the Proberts and for the old noblesse of France. It would not have occurred to the girl that such things need have been said as a mere garniture. Her lover, whose life had been surrounded with garniture and who therefore might have been expected not to notice it, had a fresh sense of it now: he reflected that manner might be a very misleading symbol, might cover pitfalls and bottomless gulfs, when it had attained that perfection and corresponded so little to fact. What he had wanted was that his people should be very civil at the hotel; but with such a high standard of compliment where after all was sincerity? And without sincerity how could people get on together when it came to their settling down to common life? Then the Dossons might have surprises, and the surprises would be painful in proportion as their present innocence was great. As to the high standard itself there was no manner of doubt; it was magnificent in its way.

VIII

WHEN, on coming home the evening after his father had made the acquaintance of the Dossons, Gaston went into the room in which the old man habitually sat, Mr Probert said, laying down his book and keeping on his glasses: 'Of course you will go on living with me. You must understand that I don't consent to your going away. You will have to occupy the rooms that Susan and Alphonse had.'

Gaston observed with pleasure the transition from the conditional to the future and also the circumstance that his father was quietly reading, according to his custom when he sat at home of an evening. This proved he was not too much off the hinge. He read a great deal, and very serious books; works about the origin of things—of man, of institutions, of speech, of religion. This habit he had taken up more particularly since the circle of his social life had grown so much smaller. He sat there alone, turning his pages softly, contentedly, with the lamplight shining on his refined old head and embroidered dressing-gown. Formerly he was out every night in the week—Gaston was perfectly aware that to many dull people he must even have appeared a little frivolous. He was essentially a social animal, and indeed—except perhaps poor Jane, in her damp old castle in Brittany—they were all social animals. That was doubtless part of the reason why the family had acclimatised itself in France. They had affinities with a society of conversation; they liked general talk and old high *salons*, slightly tarnished and dim, containing precious relics, where there was a circle round the fire and winged words flew about and there was always some clever person before the chimney-piece, holding or challenging the rest. That figure, Gaston knew, especially in the days before he could see for himself, had very often been his father, the lightest and most amiable specimen of the type that liked to take possession of the hearthrug. People left it to him; he was so transparent, like a glass screen, and he never triumphed in argument. His word on most subjects was not felt to be the last (it was usually not more conclusive than a shrugging, inarticulate resignation, an 'Ah, you know, what will you have?'); but he had been none the less a part of the essence of some dozen good houses, most of them over the river, in the conservative *faubourg*, and several to-day emptied receptacles, extinguished fires. They made up Mr Probert's world—a world not too small for him and yet not too large, though some of them supposed themselves to be very great institutions. Gaston knew the succession of events that had helped to make a difference, the most salient of which were the death of his brother, the death of his mother, and above all perhaps the extinction of Mme de Marignac, to whom the old gentleman used still to go three or four evenings out of the seven and sometimes even in the morning besides. Gaston was well aware what a place she had held in his father's life and affection, how they had grown up together (her people had been friends of his grandfather when that fine old Southern worthy came, a widower with a young son and several negroes, to take his pleasure in Paris in the time of Louis Philippe), and how much she had had to do with marrying his sisters. He was not ignorant that her friendship and all its exertions were often mentioned as explaining their position, so remarkable in a society in which they had begun after all as outsiders. But he would have guessed, even if he had not been told, what his father said to that. To offer the Proberts a position was to carry water to the fountain; they had not left their own behind them in Carolina; it had been large enough to stretch across the sea. As to what it was in Carolina there was no need of being explicit. This adoptive Parisian was by nature presupposing, but he was admirably gentle (that was why they let him talk to them before the fire—he was such a sympathising oracle), and after the death of his wife and of Mme de Marignac, who had been *her* friend too, he was gentler than before. Gaston had been able to see that it made him care less for everything (except indeed the true faith, to which he drew still closer), and this increase of indifference doubtless helped to explain his collapse in relation to common Americans.

'We shall be thankful for any rooms you will give us,' the young man said. 'We shall fill out the house a little, and won't that be rather an improvement, shrunken as you and I have become?'

'You will fill it out a good deal, I suppose, with Mr Dosson and the other girl.'

'Ah, Francie won't give up her father and sister, certainly; and what should you think of her if she did? But they are not intrusive; they are essentially modest people; they won't put themselves upon us. They have great natural discretion.'

'Do you answer for that? Susan does; she is always assuring one of it,' Mr Probert said. 'The father has so much that he wouldn't even speak to me.'

'He didn't know what to say to you.'

'How then shall I know what to say to him?'

'Ah, you always know!' Gaston exclaimed.

'How will that help us if he doesn't know what to answer?'

'You will draw him out—he is full of *bonhomie*.'

'Well, I won't quarrel with your *bonhomme* (if he's silent—there are much worse faults), nor even with the fat young lady, though she is evidently vulgar. It is not for ourselves I am afraid; it's for them. They will be very unhappy.'

'Never, never!' said Gaston. 'They are too simple. They are not morbid. And don't you like Francie? You haven't told me so,' he added in a moment.

'She says "Parus", my dear boy.'

'Ah, to Susan too that seemed the principal obstacle. But she has got over it. I mean Susan has got over the obstacle. We shall make her speak French; she has a capital disposition for it; her French is already almost as good as her English.'

'That oughtn't to be difficult. What will you have? Of course she is very pretty and I'm sure she is good. But

I won't tell you she is a marvel, because you must remember (you young fellows think your own point of view and your own experience everything), that I have seen beauties without number. I have known the most charming women of our time—women of an order to which Miss Francie, *con rispetto parlando*, will never begin to belong. I'm difficult about women—how can I help it? Therefore when you pick up a little American girl at an inn and bring her to us as a miracle, I feel how standards alter. *J'ai vu mieux que ça, mon cher.* However, I accept everything to-day, as you know; when once one has lost one's enthusiasm everything is the same, and one might as well perish by the sword as by famine.'

'I hoped she would fascinate you on the spot,' Gaston remarked, rather ruefully.

' "Fascinate"—the language you fellows use!'

'Well, she will yet.'

'She will never know at least that she doesn't: I will promise you that,' said Mr Probert.

'Ah, be sincere with her, father—she's worth it!' his son broke out.

When the old gentleman took that tone, the tone of vast experience and a fastidiousness justified by ineffable recollections, Gaston was more provoked than he could say, though he was also considerably amused, for he had a good while since made up his mind that there was an element of stupidity in it. It was fatuous to square one's self so serenely in the absence of a sense: so far from being fine it was gross not to *feel* Francie Dosson. He thanked

God *he* did. He didn't know what old frumps his father might have frequented (the style of 1830, with long curls in front, a vapid simper, a Scotch plaid dress and a body, in a point suggestive of twenty whalebones, coming down to the knees), but he could remember Mme de Marignac's Tuesdays and Thursdays and Fridays, with Sundays and other days thrown in, and the taste that prevailed in that *milieu*: the books they admired, the verses they read and recited, the pictures, great heaven! they thought good, and the three busts of the lady of the house, in different corners (as a Diana, a Druidess and a *Croyante*: her shoulders were supposed to make up for her head), effigies which to-day—even the least bad, Canova's— would draw down a public castigation upon their authors.

'And what else is she worth?' Mr Probert asked, after a momentary hesitation.

'How do you mean, what else?'

'Her immense prospects, that's what Susan has been putting forward. Susan's insistence on them was mainly what brought over Jane. Do you mind my speaking of them?'

Gaston was obliged to recognise, privately, the importance of Jane's having been brought over, but he hated to hear it spoken of as if he were under an obligation to it. 'To whom, sir?' he asked.

'Oh, only to you.'

'You can't do less than Mr Dosson. As I told you, he waived the question of money and he was superb. We can't be more mercenary than he.'

'He waived the question of his own, you mean?' said Mr Probert.

'Yes, and of yours. But it will be all right.' The young man flattered himself that that was as far as he was willing to go, in the way of bribery.

'Well, it's your affair—or your sisters',' his father returned. 'It's their idea that it will be all right.'

'I should think they would be weary of chattering!' Gaston exclaimed, impatiently.

Mr Probert looked at him a moment with a vague surprise, but he only said, 'I think they are. But the period of discussion is over. We have taken the jump.' He added, in a moment, as if from the desire to say something more conciliatory: 'Alphonse and Maxime are quite of your opinion.'

'Of my opinion?'

'That she is charming.'

'Confound them, then, I'm not of theirs!' The form of this rejoinder was childishly perverse, and it made Mr Probert stare again; but it belonged to one of the reasons for which his children regarded him as an old darling that Gaston could feel after an instant that he comprehended it. The old man said nothing, but took up his book, and his son, who had been standing before the fire, went out of the room. His abstention from protest at Gaston's petulance was the more commendable as he was capable, for his part, of thinking it important that *ces messieurs* should like the little girl at the hotel. Gaston was not, and it would have seemed to him a proof that he was in servitude indeed if he had accepted such an assurance as that as if it mattered. This was especially the case as his father's mention of the approval of two of his brothers-in-law appeared to point to a possible disapproval on the part of the third. Francie's lover cared as little whether she displeased M. de Brécourt as he cared whether she displeased Maxime and Raoul. The old gentleman continued to read, and in a few moments Gaston came back. He had expressed surprise, just before, that his sisters should have found so much to discuss in the idea of his marriage, but he looked at his father now with an air of having more to say—an intimation that the subject must not be considered as exhausted. 'It seems rather odd to me that you should all appear to accept the step I am about to take as a sort of disagreeable necessity, when I myself hold that I have been so exceedingly fortunate.'

Mr Probert lowered his book accommodatingly and rested his eyes upon the fire. 'You won't be content till we are enthusiastic. She seems a good girl, certainly, and in that you are fortunate.'

'I don't think you can tell me what would be better—what you would have preferred,' said the young man.

'What I would have preferred? In the first place you must remember that I was not madly impatient to see you married.'

'I can imagine that, and yet I can't imagine that, as things have turned out, you shouldn't be struck with the felicity. To get something so charming, and to get it of our own species.'

'Of our own species? *Tudieu!*' said Mr Probert looking up.

'Surely it is infinitely fresher and more amusing for me to marry an American. There's a dreariness in the way we have Gallicised.'

'Against Americans I have nothing to say; some of them are the best thing the world contains. That's precisely why one can choose. They are far from being all like that.'

'Like what, dear father?'

'*Comme ces gens-là.* You know that if they were French, being otherwise what they are, one wouldn't look at them.'

'Indeed one would; they would be such curiosities.'

'Well, perhaps they are sufficiently so as it is,' said Mr Probert, with a little conclusive sigh.

'Yes, let them pass for that. They will surprise you.'

'Not too much, I hope!' cried the old man, opening his volume again.

It will doubtless not startle the reader to learn that the complexity of things among the Proberts was such as to make it impossible for Gaston to proceed to the celebration of his nuptials, with all the needful circumstances of material preparation and social support, before some three months should have expired. He chafed however but moderately at the delay, for he reflected that it would give Francie time to endear herself to his whole circle. It would also have advantages for the Dossons; it would enable them to establish by simple but effective arts the *modus vivendi* with that rigid body. It would in short help every one to get used to everything. Mr Dosson's designs and Delia's took no articulate form; what was mainly clear to Gaston was that his future wife's relatives had as yet no sense of disconnection. He knew that Mr Dosson would do whatever Delia liked and that Delia would like to 'start' her sister. Whether or no she expected to be present at the finish, she had a definite purpose of seeing the beginning of the race. Mr Probert notified Mr Dosson of what he proposed to 'do' for his son, and Mr Dosson appeared more amused than anything else at the news. He announced, in return, no intentions in regard to Francie, and his queer silence was the cause of another convocation of the house of Probert. Here Mme de Brécourt's valorous spirit won another victory; she maintained, as she informed her brother, that there was no possible policy but a policy of confidence. 'Lord help us, is that what they call confidence?' the young man exclaimed, guessing the way they all looked at each other; and he wondered how they would look next at poor Mr Dosson. Fortunately he could always fall back, for reassurance, upon that revelation of their perfect manners; though indeed he thoroughly knew that on the day they should really attempt interference—make a row which might render him helpless and culminate in a rupture—their courtesy would show its finest flower.

Mr Probert's property was altogether in the United States: he resembled various other persons to whom American impressions are mainly acceptable in the form of dividends. The manner in which he desired to benefit his son on the occasion of the latter's marriage rendered certain visitations and reinvestments necessary in that country. It had long been his conviction that his affairs needed looking into; they had gone on for years and years without an overhauling. He had thought of going back to see, but now he was too old and too tired and the effort was impossible. There was nothing for it but for Gaston to go, and go quickly, though the moment was rather awkward. The idea was communicated to him and the necessity accepted; then the plan was relinquished: it seemed such a pity he should not wait till after his marriage, when he would be able to take Francie with him. Francie would be such an introducer. This postponement would have taken effect had it not suddenly come out that Mr Dosson himself wanted to go for a few weeks, in consequence of some news (it was a matter of business), that he had unexpectedly received. It was further revealed that that course presented difficulties, for he could not leave his daughters alone, especially in such a situation. Not only would such a proceeding have given scandal to the Proberts, but Gaston learned, with a good deal of surprise and not a little amusement, that Delia, in consequence of peculiar changes now wrought in her view of things, would have felt herself obliged to protest on the score of propriety. He called her attention to the fact that nothing would be more simple than, in the interval, for Francie to go and stay with Susan or Margaret; Delia herself in that case would be free to accompany her father.

But this young lady declared that nothing would induce her to quit the European continent until she had seen her sister through, and Gaston shrank from proposing that she too should spend five weeks in the Place Beauvau or the Rue de Lille. Moreover he was startled, he was a good deal mystified, by the perverse, unsociable way in which Francie asserted that, as yet, she would not lend herself to any staying. *After*, if he liked, but not till then. And she would not at the moment give the reasons of her refusal; it was only very positive and even quite passionate.

All this left her intended no alternative but to say to Mr Dosson, 'I am not such a fool as I look. If you will coach me properly, and trust me, I will rush across and transact your business as well as my father's.' Strange as it appeared, Francie could resign herself to this separation from her lover—it would last six or seven weeks—rather than accept the hospitality of his sisters. Mr Dosson trusted him; he said to him, 'Well, sir, you've got a big brain,' at the end of a morning they spent with papers and pencils; upon which Gaston made his preparations to sail. Before he left Paris Francie, to do her justice, confided to him that her objection to going in such an intimate way even to Mme de Brécourt's had been founded on a fear that in close quarters she would do something that would make them all despise her. Gaston replied, in the first place, that this was gammon and in the second he wanted to know if she expected never to be in close quarters with her new kinsfolk. 'Ah, yes, but then it will be safer—we shall be married!' she returned. This little incident occurred three days before the young man started; but what happened just the evening previous was that, stopping for a last word at the Hôtel de l'Univers et de Cheltenham on his way to take the night express to London (he was to sail from Liverpool), he found Mr George Flack sitting in the red-satin saloon. The correspondent of the *Reverberator* had come back.

IX

Mr Flack's relations with his old friends did not, after his appearance in Paris, take on that familiarity and frequency which had marked their intercourse a year before: he let them know frankly that he could easily see the situation was quite different. They had got into the high set and they didn't care about the past: he alluded to the past as if it had been rich in mutual vows, in pledges now repudiated. 'What's the matter? Won't you come round there with us some day?' Mr Dosson asked; not having perceived for himself any reason why the young journalist should not be a welcome and congruous figure in the Cours la Reine.

Delia wanted to know what Mr Flack was talking about: didn't he know a lot of people that they didn't know and wasn't it natural they should have their own society? The young man's treatment of the question was humorous, and it was with Delia that the discussion mainly went forward. When he maintained that the Dossons had 'shed' him, Mr Dosson exclaimed, 'Well, I guess you'll grow again!' And Francie observed that it was no use for him to pose as a martyr, inasmuch as he knew perfectly well that with all the celebrated people he saw and the way he flew round he had the most enchanting time. She was aware she was a good deal less accessible than she had been the previous spring, for Mesdames de Brécourt and de Cliché (the former much more than the latter) took a considerable number of her hours. In spite of her protest to Gaston against a premature intimacy with his sisters, she spent whole days in their company (they had so much to tell her about what her new life would be, and it was generally very pleasant), and she thought it would be nice if in these intervals he should give himself to her father and even to Delia as he used to do.

But the flaw of a certain insincerity in Mr Flack's nature seemed to be established by his present tendency to rare visits. He evidently did not care for her father for himself, and though Mr Dosson was the least querulous of men she divined that he suspected their old companion had fallen away. There were no more wanderings in public places, no more tryings of new cafés. Mr Dosson used to look sometimes as he had looked of old when George Flack 'located' them somewhere; as if he expected to see their sharp cicerone rushing back to them, with his drab overcoat flying in the wind; but this expectation usually died away. He missed Gaston because Gaston this winter had so often ordered his dinner for him, and his society was not sought by the count and the marquis, whose mastery of English was small and their other distractions great. Mr Probert, it was true, had shown something of a fraternising spirit; he had come twice to the hotel, since his son's departure, and he had said, smiling and reproachful, 'You neglect us, you neglect us!' Mr Dosson had not understood what he meant by this till Delia explained after the visitor withdrew, and even then the remedy for the neglect, administered two or three days later, had not borne any particular fruit. Mr Dosson called alone, instructed by his daughter, in the Cours la Reine, but Mr Probert was not at home. He only left a card, on which Delia had superscribed in advance the words 'So sorry!' Her father had told her he would give the card if she wanted, but he would have nothing to do with the writing. There was a discussion as to whether Mr Probert's remark was an allusion to a deficiency of politeness on the article of his sons-in-law. Ought not Mr Dosson perhaps to call personally, and not simply through the medium of the visits paid by his daughters to their wives, on Messieurs de Brécourt and de Cliché? Once, when this subject came up in George Flack's presence, the old man said he would go round if Mr Flack would accompany him. 'All right!' said Mr Flack, and this conception became a reality, with the accidental abatement that the objects of the demonstration were absent. 'Suppose they get in?' Delia had said lugubriously to her sister.

'Well, what if they do?' Francie asked.

'Why, the count and the marquis won't be interested in Mr Flack.'

'Well then, perhaps he will be interested in them. He can write something about them. They will like that.'

'Do you think they would?' Delia demanded in solemn dubiousness.

'Why, yes, if he should say fine things.'

'They do like fine things,' said Delia. 'They get off so many themselves. Only the way Mr Flack does it—it's a different style.'

'Well, people like to be praised in any style.'

'That's so,' Delia rejoined, musingly.

One afternoon, coming in about three o'clock, Mr Flack found Francie alone. She had expressed a wish, after luncheon, for a couple of hours of independence: she intended to write to Gaston, and having accidentally missed a post promised herself that her letter should be of double its usual length. Her companions respected her desire for solitude, Mr Dosson taking himself off to his daily session in the reading-room of the American bank and Delia (the girls had now a luxurious coach at their command) driving away to the dressmaker's, a frequent errand, to superintend and urge forward the progress of her sister's wedding-clothes. Francie was not skilled in composition; she wrote slowly and in addressing her lover had a painful sense of literary responsibility. Her father and Delia had a theory that when she shut herself up that way she poured forth wonderful pages—it was part of her high cultivation. At any rate, when George Flack was ushered in she was still bending over her blotting-book on one of the gilded tables and there was an inkstain on her pointed forefinger. It was no disloyalty to Gaston but only at the most a sense of weariness in regard to the epistolary form that made her glad to see her visitor. She didn't know how to finish her letter; but Mr Flack seemed in a manner to terminate it.

'I wouldn't have ventured to propose this, but I guess I can do with it, now it's come,' the young man announced.

'What can you do with?' she asked, wiping her pen.

'Well, this happy chance. Just you and me together.'

'I don't know what it's a chance for.'

'Well, for me to be a little less miserable for a quarter of an hour. It makes me so to see you look so happy.'

'It makes you miserable?'

'You ought to understand, when I say something magnanimous.' And settling himself on the sofa Mr Flack continued, 'Well, how do you get on without Mr Probert?'

'Very well indeed, thank you.'

The tone in which the girl spoke was not an encouragement to free pleasantry, so that if Mr Flack continued his inquiries it was in a guarded and respectful manner. He was eminently capable of reflecting that it was not in his interest to strike her as indiscreet and profane; he only wanted to appear friendly, worthy of confidence. At the same time he was not averse to the idea that she should still perceive in him a certain sense of injury, and that could be indicated only by a touch of bitterness here and there. The injury, the bitterness might make her pity him. 'Well, you are in the *grand monde*, I suppose,' he resumed at last, not with an air of derision but resignedly, sympathetically.

'Oh, I'm not in anything; I'm just where I've always been.'

'I'm sorry; I hoped you would tell me about it,' said Mr Flack, gravely.

'You think too much of that. What do you want to know about it for?'

'Dear Miss Francie, a poor devil of a journalist who has to get his living by studying up things, he has to think too much, sometimes, in order to think, or at any rate to do, enough. We find out what we can—as we can.'

Francie listened to this as if it had had the note of pathos. 'What do you want to study up?'

'Everything! I take in everything. It all depends on my opportunity. I try and learn—I try and improve. Every one has something to tell, and I listen and watch and make my profit of it. I hoped *you* would have something to tell. I don't believe but what you've seen a good deal of new life. You won't pretend they haven't roped you in, charming as you are.'

'Do you mean if they've been kind to me? They've been very kind,' Francie said. 'They want to do even more than I'll let them.'

'Ah, why won't you let them?' George Flack asked, almost coaxingly.

'Well, I do,' the girl went on. 'You can't resist them, really; they have such lovely ways.'

'I should like to hear you talk about their ways,' her companion observed, after a silence.

'Oh, I could talk enough if once I were to begin. But I don't see why it should interest you.'

'Don't I care immensely for everything that concerns you? Didn't I tell you that once?'

'You're foolish if you do, and you would be foolish to say it again,' Francie replied.

'Oh, I don't want to say anything, I've had my lesson. But I could listen to you all day.' Francie gave an exclamation of impatience and incredulity, and Mr Flack pursued: 'Don't you remember what you told me that time we had that talk at Saint-Germain, on the terrace? You said I might remain your friend.'

'Well, that's all right,' said the girl.

'Then ain't we interested in the development of our friends—in their impressions, their transformations, their adventures? Especially a person like me, who has got to know life—who has got to know the world.'

'Do you mean to say I could teach you about life?' Francie demanded.

'About some kinds, certainly. You know a lot of people whom it's difficult to get at unless one takes some extraordinary measures, as you have done.'

'What do you mean? What measures have I taken?'

'Well, they have—to get hold of you—and it's the same thing. Pouncing on you, to secure you; I call that energetic, and don't you think I ought to know?' asked Mr Flack, smiling. 'I thought *I* was energetic, but they got ahead of me. They're a society apart, and they must be very curious.'

'Yes, they're curious,' Francie admitted, with a little sigh. Then she inquired: 'Do you want to put them in the paper?'

George Flack hesitated a moment; the air of the question was so candid, suggested so complete an exemption from prejudice. 'Oh, I'm very careful about what I put in the paper. I want everything, as I told you; don't you remember the sketch I gave you of my ideals? But I want it in a certain particular way. If I can't get it in the shape I like it I don't want it at all; genuine, first-hand information, straight from the tap, is what I'm after. I don't want to hear what some one or other thinks that some one or other was told that some one or other repeated; and above all I don't want to print it. There's plenty of that flowing in, and the best part of the job is to keep it out. People just yearn to come in; they're dying to, all over the place; there's the biggest crowd at the door. But I say to them: "You've got to do something first, then I'll see; or at any rate you've got to *be* something!"'

'We sometimes see the *Reverberator*; you have some fine pieces,' Francie replied.

'Sometimes, only? Don't they send it to your father—

the weekly edition? I thought I had fixed that,' said George Flack.

'I don't know; it's usually lying round. But Delia reads it more than I; she reads pieces aloud. I like to read books; I read as many as I can.'

'Well, it's all literature,' said Mr Flack; 'it's all the press, the great institution of our time. Some of the finest books have come out first in the papers. It's the history of the age.'

'I see you've got the same aspirations,' Francie remarked kindly.

'The same aspirations?'

'Those you told me about that day at Saint-Germain.'

'Oh, I keep forgetting that I ever broke out to you that way; everything is so changed.'

'Are you the proprietor of the paper now?' the girl went on, determined not to notice this sentimental allusion.

'What do you care? It wouldn't even be delicate in me to tell you; for I *do* remember the way you said you would try and get your father to help me. Don't say you've forgotten it, because you almost made me cry. Any way, that isn't the sort of help I want now and it wasn't the sort of help I meant to ask you for then. I want sympathy and interest; I want someone to whisper once in a while—"Courage, courage; you'll come out all right." You see I'm a working man and I don't pretend to be anything else,' Mr Flack went on. 'I don't live on the accumulations of my ancestors. What I have I earn—

what I am I've fought for: I'm a *travailleur*, as they say here. I rejoice in it; but there is one dark spot in it, all the same.'

'And what is that?' asked Francie.

'That it makes you ashamed of me.'

'Oh, how can you say?' And she got up, as if a sense of oppression, of vague discomfort, had come over her. Her visitor made her fidgety.

'You wouldn't be ashamed to go round with me?'

'Round where?'

'Well, anywhere: just to have one more walk. The very last.' George Flack had got up too and he stood there looking at her with his bright eyes, with his hands in the pockets of his overcoat. As she hesitated he continued, 'Then I'm not such a friend after all.'

Francie rested her eyes for a moment on the carpet; then, raising them—'Where should you like to go?'

'You could render me a service—a real service—without any inconvenience, probably, to yourself. Isn't your portrait finished?'

'Yes, but he won't give it up.'

'Who won't give it up?'

'Why, Mr Waterlow. He wants to keep it near him to look at it in case he should take a fancy to change it. But I hope he won't change it—it's so pretty as it is!' Francie declared, smiling.

'I hear it's magnificent, and I want to see it,' said George Flack.

'Then why don't you go?'

'I'll go if you'll take me; that's the service you can render me.'

'Why, I thought you went everywhere—into the palaces of kings!' Francie cried.

'I go where I'm welcome, not where I'm not. I don't want to push into that studio alone; he doesn't like me. Oh, you needn't protest,' the young man went on; 'if one is sensitive one is sensitive. I feel those things in the shade of a tone of voice. He doesn't like newspaper-men. Some people don't, you know. I ought to tell you that frankly.'

Francie considered again, but looking this time at her visitor. 'Why, if it hadn't been for you'—I am afraid she said 'hadn't have been'—'I never would have sat to him.'

Mr Flack smiled at her in silence for an instant. 'If it hadn't been for me I think you never would have met your future husband.'

'Perhaps not,' said Francie; and suddenly she blushed red, rather to her companion's surprise.

'I only say that to remind you that after all I have a right to ask you to show me this one little favour. Let me drive with you to-morrow, or next day or any day, to the Avenue de Villiers, and I shall regard myself as amply repaid. With you I sha'n't be afraid to go in, for you have a right to take anyone you like to see your picture. It's always done.'

'Oh, the day you're afraid, Mr Flack—!' Francie exclaimed, laughing. She had been much struck by his reminder of what they all owed him; for he truly had been their initiator, the instrument, under providence, that had opened a great new interest to them, and it shocked her generosity, the intimation that he saw himself cast off or disavowed after the prize was gained. Her mind had not lingered on her personal indebtedness to him, for it was not in the nature of her mind to linger; but at present she was glad to spring quickly, at the first word, into the attitude of acknowledgment. It had the effect that simplification always has, it raised her spirits, made her merry.

'Of course I must be quite square with you,' the young man said. 'If I want to see the picture it's because I want to write about it. The whole thing will go bang into the *Reverberator*. You must understand that, in advance. I wouldn't write about it without seeing it.'

'*J'espère bien!*' said Francie, who was getting on famously with her French. 'Of course if you praise him Mr Waterlow will like it.'

'I don't know that he cares for my praise and I don't care much whether *he* likes it or not. If you like it, that's the principal thing.'

'Oh, I shall be awfully proud.'

'I shall speak of you personally—I shall say you are the prettiest girl that has ever come over.'

'You may say what you like,' Francie rejoined. 'It will be immense fun to be in the newspapers. Come for me at this hour day after to-morrow.'

'You're too kind,' said George Flack, taking up his hat. He smoothed it down a moment, with his glove;

then he said—'I wonder if you will mind our going alone?'

'Alone?'

'I mean just you and me.'

'Oh, don't you be afraid! Father and Delia have seen it about thirty times.'

'That will be delightful, then. And it will help me to feel, more than anything else could make me do, that we are still old friends. I'll come at 3.15,' Mr Flack went on, but without even yet taking his departure. He asked two or three questions about the hotel, whether it were as good as last year and there were many people in it and they could keep their rooms warm; then, suddenly, in a different order and scarcely waiting for the girl's answer, he said: 'And now, for instance, are they very bigoted? That's one of the things I should like to know.'

'Very bigoted?'

'Ain't they tremendous Catholics—always talking about the Holy Father, and that sort of thing? I mean Mr Probert, the old gentleman,' Mr Flack added. 'And those ladies, and all the rest of them.'

'They are very religious,' said Francie. 'They are the most religious people I ever saw. They just adore the Holy Father. They know him personally quite well. They are always going down to Rome.'

'And do they mean to introduce you to him?'

'How do you mean, to introduce me?'

'Why, to make you a Catholic, to take you also down to Rome.'

'Oh, we are going to Rome for our *voyage de noces*!' said Francie, gaily. 'Just for a peep.'

'And won't you have to have a Catholic marriage? They won't consent to a Protestant one.'

'We are going to have a lovely one, just like one that Mme de Brécourt took me to see at the Madeleine.'

'And will it be at the Madeleine, too?'

'Yes, unless we have it at Notre Dame.'

'And how will your father and sister like that?'

'Our having it at Notre Dame?'

'Yes, or at the Madeleine. Your not having it at the American church.'

'Oh, Delia wants it at the best place,' said Francie, simply. Then she added: 'And you know father ain't much on religion.'

'Well now, that's what I call a genuine fact, the sort I was talking about,' Mr Flack replied. Whereupon he at last took himself off, repeating that he would come in two days later, at 3.15 sharp.

Francie gave an account of his visit to her sister, on the return of the latter young lady, and mentioned the agreement they had come to in relation to the drive. Delia, at this, looked grave, asseverating that she didn't know that it was right ('as' it was right, Delia usually said,) that Francie should be so intimate with other gentlemen after she was engaged.

'Intimate? You wouldn't think it's very intimate if you were to see me!' cried Francie, laughing.

'I'm sure I don't want to see you,' Delia declared; and

her sister, becoming strenuous, authoritative, went on: 'Delia Dosson, do you realise that if it hadn't been for Mr Flack we would never have had that picture, and that if it hadn't been for that picture I should never have got engaged?'

'It would have been better if you hadn't, if that's the way you are going to behave. Nothing would induce me to go with you.'

This was what suited Francie; but she was nevertheless struck by Delia's rigidity. 'I'm only going to take him to see Mr Waterlow,' she explained.

'Has he become all of a sudden too shy to go alone?'

'Well, you know Mr Waterlow doesn't like him—and he has made him feel it. You know Gaston told us so.'

'He told us *he* couldn't bear him; that's what he told us,' said Delia.

'All the more reason I should be kind to him. Why, Delia, do realise,' Francie went on.

'That's just what I do,' returned the elder girl; 'but things that are very different from those you want me to. You have queer reasons.'

'I have others too that you may like better. He wants to put a piece in the paper about it.'

'About your picture?'

'Yes, and about me. All about the whole thing.'

Delia stared a moment. 'Well, I hope it will be a good one!' she said with a little sigh of resignation, as if she were accepting the burden of a still larger fate.

X

WHEN Francie, two days later, passed with Mr Flack into Charles Waterlow's studio she found Mme de Cliché before the great canvas. She was pleased by every sign that the Proberts took an interest in her, and this was a considerable symptom, Gaston's second sister's coming all that way (she lived over by the Invalides) to look at the portrait once more. Francie knew she had seen it at an earlier stage; the work had excited curiosity and discussion among the Proberts from the first of their making her acquaintance and they went into considerations about it which had not occurred to the original and her companions—frequently (as we know) as these good people had conversed on the subject. Gaston had told her that opinions differed much in the family as to the merit of the work and that Margaret, precisely, had gone so far as to say that it might be a masterpiece of tone but it didn't make her look like a lady. His father on the other hand had no objection to offer to the character in which it represented her but he didn't think it well painted. '*Regardez-moi ça, et ça, et ça, je vous demande!*' he had exclaimed, making little dashes at the canvas, toward spots that appeared to him eccentric, with his glove, on occasions when the artist was not at hand. The Proberts always fell into French when they spoke on a question of art. 'Poor dear papa, he only understands *le vieux jeu!*' Gaston had explained, and he had still further to expound what he meant by the old game. The novelty of Charles Waterlow's game had already been a mystification to Mr Probert.

Francie remembered now (she had forgotten it) that Margaret de Cliché had told her she meant to come again. She hoped the marquise thought by this time that, on canvas at least, she looked a little more like a lady. Mme de Cliché smiled at her at any rate and kissed her, as if in fact there could be no mistake. She smiled also at Mr Flack, on Francie's introducing him, and only looked grave when, after she had asked where the others were— the papa and the *grande sœur*—the girl replied that she hadn't the least idea: her party consisted only of herself and Mr Flack. Then Mme de Cliché became very stern indeed—assumed an aspect that brought back Francie's sense that she was the individual, among all Gaston's belongings, who had pleased her least from the first. Mme de Douves was superficially more formidable but with her the second impression was most comforting. It was just this second impression of the marquise that was not. There were perhaps others behind it but the girl had not yet arrived at them. Mr Waterlow might not have been very fond of Mr Flack, but he was none the less perfectly civil to him, and took much trouble to show him all the work that he had in hand, dragging out canvases, changing lights, taking him off to see things at the other end of the great room. While the two gentlemen were at a distance Mme de Cliché expressed to Francie the confidence that she would allow her to see her home: on which

Francie replied that she was not going home, she was
going somewhere else with Mr Flack. And she explained,
as if it simplified the matter, that this gentleman was an
editor.

Her interlocutress echoed the term and Francie de-
veloped her explanation. He was not the only editor, but
one of the many editors, of a great American paper. He
was going to publish an article about her picture. Gaston
knew him perfectly; it was Mr Flack who had been the
cause of Gaston's being presented to her. Mme de Cliché
looked across at him as if the inadequacy of the cause projected an unfavourable light upon the effect; she inquired
whether Francie thought Gaston would like her to drive
about Paris alone with an editor. 'I'm sure I don't know.
I never asked him!' said Francie. 'He ought to want me
to be polite to a person who did so much for us.' Soon
after this Mme de Cliché withdrew, without looking
afresh at Mr Flack, though he stood in her path as she
approached the door. She did not kiss our young lady
again, and the girl observed that her leave-taking consisted of the simple words, 'Adieu, mademoiselle.' She
had already perceived that in proportion as the Proberts
became majestic they had recourse to French.

She and Mr Flack remained in the studio but a short
time longer; and when they were seated in the carriage
again, at the door (they had come in Mr Dosson's open
landau), her companion said, 'And now where shall we
go?' He spoke as if on their way from the hotel he had
not touched upon the pleasant vision of a little turn in

the Bois. He had insisted then that the day was made on purpose, the air full of spring. At present he seemed to wish to give himself the pleasure of making his companion choose that particular alternative. But she only answered rather impatiently:

'Wherever you like, wherever you like.' And she sat there swaying her parasol, looking about her, giving no order.

'Au Bois,' said George Flack to the coachman, leaning back on the soft cushions. For a few moments after the carriage had taken its easy elastic start they were silent; but presently he went on, 'Was that lady one of your relations?'

'Do you mean one of Mr Probert's? She is his sister.'

'Is there any particular reason in that why she shouldn't say good-morning to me?'

'She didn't want you to remain with me. She wanted to carry me off.'

'What has she got against me?' asked Mr Flack.

Francie seemed to consider a little. 'Oh, it's these French ideas.'

'Some of them are very base,' said her companion.

The girl made no rejoinder; she only turned her eyes to right and left, admiring the splendid day, the shining city. The great architectural vista was fair: the tall houses, with their polished shop-fronts, their balconies, their signs with accented letters, seemed to make a glitter of gilt and crystal as they rose into the sunny air. The colour of everything was cool and pretty and the sound of everything gay; the sense of a costly spectacle was everywhere. 'Well, I like Paris, anyway!' Francie exclaimed at last.

'It's lucky for you, since you've got to live here.'

'I haven't got to, there's no obligation. We haven't settled anything about that.'

'Hasn't that lady settled it for you?'

'Yes, very likely she has,' said Francie, placidly. 'I don't like her so well as the others.'

'You like the others very much?'

'Of course I do. So would you if they had made so much of you.'

'That one at the studio didn't make much of me, certainly.'

'Yes, she's the most haughty,' said Francie.

'Well, what is it all about?' Mr Flack inquired. 'Who are they, anyway?'

'Oh, it would take me three hours to tell you,' the girl replied, laughing. 'They go back a thousand years.'

'Well, we've got a thousand years—I mean three hours.' And George Flack settled himself more on his cushions and inhaled the pleasant air. 'I do enjoy this drive, Miss Francie,' he went on. 'It's many a day since I've been to the Bois. I don't fool round much among the trees.'

Francie replied candidly that for her too the occasion was very agreeable, and Mr Flack pursued, looking round him with a smile, irrelevantly and cheerfully: 'Yes, these French ideas! I don't see how you can stand them. Those they have about young ladies are horrid.'

'Well, they tell me you like them better after you are married.'

'Why, after they are married they're worse—I mean the ideas. Every one knows that.'

'Well, they can make you like anything, the way they talk,' Francie said.

'And do they talk a great deal?'

'Well, I should think so. They don't do much else, and they talk about the queerest things—things I never heard of.'

'Ah, that I'll engage!' George Flack exclaimed.

'Of course I have had most conversation with Mr. Probert.'

'The old gentleman?'

'No, very little with him. I mean with Gaston. But it's not he that has told me most—it's Mme de Brécourt. She relates and relates—it's very interesting. She has told me all their histories, all their troubles and complications.'

'Complications?'

'That's what she calls them. It seems very different from America. It's just like a story—they have such strange feelings. But there are things you can see—without being told.'

'What sort of things?'

'Well, like Mme de Cliché's—' But Francie paused, as if for a word.

'Do you mean her complications?'

'Yes, and her husband's. She has terrible ones. That's

why one must forgive her if she is rather peculiar. She is very unhappy.'

'Do you mean through her husband?'

'Yes, he likes other ladies better. He flirts with Mme de Brives.'

'Mme de Brives?'

'Yes, she's lovely,' said Francie. 'She isn't very young, but she's fearfully attractive. And he used to go every day to have tea with Mme de Villepreux. Mme de Cliché can't bear Mme de Villepreux.'

'Lord, what a low character he must be!' George Flack exclaimed.

'Oh, his mother was very bad. That was one thing they had against the marriage.'

'Who had?—against what marriage?'

'When Maggie Probert became engaged.'

'Is that what they call her—Maggie?'

'Her brother does; but every one else calls her Margot. Old Mme de Cliché had a horrid reputation. Every one hated her.'

'Except those, I suppose, who liked her too much. And who is Mme de Villepreux?'

'She's the daughter of Mme de Marignac.'

'And who is Mme de Marignac?'

'Oh, she's dead,' said Francie. 'She used to be a great friend of Mr Probert—of Gaston's father.'

'He used to go to tea with her?'

'Almost every day. Susan says he has never been the same since her death.'

'Ah, poor man! And who is Susan?'

'Why, Mme de Brécourt. Mr Probert just loved Mme de Marignac. Mme de Villepreux isn't so nice as her mother. She was brought up with the Proberts, like a sister, and now she carries on with Maxime.'

'With Maxime?'

'That's M. de Cliché.'

'Oh, I see—I see!' murmured George Flack, responsively. They had reached the top of the Champs Elysées and were passing below the wondrous arch to which that gentle eminence forms a pedestal and which looks down even on splendid Paris from its immensity and across at the vain mask of the Tuileries and the river-moated Louvre and the twin towers of Notre Dame, painted blue by the distance. The confluence of carriages—a sounding stream, in which our friends became engaged—rolled into the large avenue leading to the Bois de Boulogne. Mr Flack evidently enjoyed the scene; he gazed about him at their neighbours, at the villas and gardens on either hand; he took in the prospect of the far-stretching brown boskages and smooth alleys of the wood, of the hour that they had yet to spend there, of the rest of Francie's artless prattle, of the place near the lake where they could alight and walk a little; even of the bench where they might sit down. 'I see, I see,' he repeated with appreciation. 'You make me feel quite as if I were in the *grand monde*.'

XI

ONE day, at noon, shortly before the time for which
Gaston had announced his return, a note was brought to
Francie from Mme de Brécourt. It caused her some agita-
tion, though it contained a clause intended to guard her
against vain fears. 'Please come to me the moment you
have received this—I have sent the carriage. I will explain when you get here what I want to see you about.
Nothing has happened to Gaston. We are all here.' The
coupé from the Place Beauvau was waiting at the door of
the hotel and the girl had but a hurried conference with
her father and sister; if conference it could be called in
which vagueness on one side encountered blankness on
the other. 'It's for something bad—something bad,' Francie said, while she tied her bonnet; though she was unable to think what it could be. Delia, who looked a good
deal scared, offered to accompany her; upon which Mr
Dosson made the first remark of a practical character in
which he had indulged in relation to his daughter's
alliance.

'No you won't—no you won't, my dear. They may
whistle for Francie, but let them see that they can't
whistle for all of us.' It was the first sign he had given of
being jealous of the dignity of the Dossons. That question
had never troubled him.

'I know what it is,' said Delia, while she arranged her
sister's garments. 'They want to talk about religion. They

have got the priests; there's some bishop, or perhaps some cardinal. They want to baptise you.'

'You'd better take a waterproof!' Francie's father called after her as she flitted away.

She wondered, rolling toward the Place Beauvau, what they were all there for; that announcement balanced against the reassurance conveyed in the phrase about Gaston. She liked them individually but in their collective form they made her uneasy. In their family parties there was always something of the tribunal. Mme de Brécourt came out to meet her in the vestibule, drawing her quickly into a small room (not the salon—Francie knew it as her hostess's 'own room', a lovely boudoir), in which, considerably to the girl's relief, the rest of the family were not assembled. Yet she guessed in a moment that they were near at hand—they were waiting. Susan looked flushed and strange; she had a queer smile; she kissed her as if she didn't know that she was doing it. She laughed as she greeted her, but her laugh was nervous; she was different every way from anything Francie had hitherto seen. By the time our young lady had perceived these things she was sitting beside her on a sofa and Mme de Brécourt had her hand, which she held so tight that it almost hurt her. Susan's eyes were in their nature salient, but on this occasion they seemed to have started out of her head.

'We are upside down—terribly agitated. A bomb has fallen into the house.'

'What's the matter—what's the matter?' Francie asked,

pale, with parted lips. She had a sudden wild idea that Gaston might have found out in America that her father had no money, had lost it all; that it had been stolen during their long absence. But would he cast her off for that?

'You must understand the closeness of our union with you from our sending for you this way—the first, the only person—in a crisis. Our joys are your joys and our indignations are yours.'

'What *is* the matter, *please?*' the girl repeated. Their 'indignations' opened up a gulf; it flashed upon her, with a shock of mortification that the idea had not come sooner, that something would have come out: a piece in the paper, from Mr Flack, about her portrait and even (a little) about herself. But that was only more mystifying; for certainly Mr Flack could only have published something pleasant—something to be proud of. Had he by some incredible perversity or treachery stated that the picture was bad, or even that *she* was? She grew dizzy, remembering how she had refused him and how little he had liked it, that day at Saint-Germain. But they had made that up over and over, especially when they sat so long on a bench together (the time they drove), in the Bois de Boulogne.

'Oh, the most awful thing; a newspaper sent this morning from America to my father—containing two horrible columns of vulgar lies and scandal about our family, about all of us, about you, about your picture, about poor Marguerite, calling her "Margot", about Maxime and Léonie de Villepreux, saying he's her lover, about all our affairs, about Gaston, about your marriage, about your sister and your dresses and your dimples, about our darling father, whose history it professes to relate, in the most ignoble, the most revolting terms. Papa's in the most awful state!' said Mme de Brécourt, panting to take breath. She had spoken with the volubility of horror and passion. 'You are outraged with us and you must suffer with us,' she went on. 'But who has done it? Who has done it? Who has done it?'

'Why, Mr Flack—Mr Flack!' Francie quickly replied. She was appalled, overwhelmed; but her foremost feeling was the wish not to appear to disavow her knowledge.

'Mr Flack? do you mean that awful person—? He ought to be shot, he ought to be burnt alive. Maxime will kill him, Maxime is in an unspeakable rage. Everything is at end, we have been served up to the rabble, we shall have to leave Paris. How could he know such things? and they are all too infamously false!' The poor woman poured forth her trouble in questions and contradictions and groans; she knew not what to ask first, against what to protest. 'Do you mean that person Marguerite saw you with at Mr Waterlow's? Oh, Francie, what has happened? She had a feeling then, a dreadful foreboding. She saw you afterwards—walking with him—in the Bois.'

'Well, I didn't see her,' the girl said.

'You were talking with him—you were too absorbed: that's what Margot says. Oh, Francie, Francie!' cried Mme de Brécourt, catching her breath.

'She tried to interfere at the studio, but I wouldn't let her. He's an old friend—a friend of my father's, and I like him very much. What my father allows, that's not for others to criticise!' Francie continued. She was frightened, extremely frightened, at her companion's air of tragedy and at the dreadful consequences she alluded to, consequences of an act she herself did not know, could not comprehend nor measure yet. But there was an instinct of bravery in her which threw her into defence—defence even of George Flack, though it was a part of her consternation that on her too he should have practised a surprise, a sort of selfish deception.

'Oh, how can you bear with such wretches—how can your father—— ? What devil has he paid to tattle to him?'

'You scare me awfully—you terrify me,' said the girl. 'I don't know what you are talking about. I haven't seen it, I don't understand it. Of course I have talked to Mr Flack.'

'Oh, Francie, don't say it—don't *say* it! Dear child, you haven't talked to him in that fashion: vulgar horrors, and such a language!' Mme de Brécourt came nearer, took both her hands now, drew her closer, seemed to plead with her. 'You shall see the paper; they have got it in the other room—the most disgusting sheet. Margot is reading it to her husband; he can't read English, if you can call it English: such a style! Papa tried to translate it to Maxime, but he couldn't, he was too sick. There is a quantity about Mme de Marignac—imagine only! And a quantity about Jeanne and Raoul and their economies in the country. When they see it in Brittany—heaven preserve us!'

Francie had turned very white; she looked for a minute at the carpet. 'And what does it say about me?'

'Some trash about your being the great American beauty, with the most odious details, and your having made a match among the "rare old exclusives". And the strangest stuff about your father—his having gone into a "store" at the age of twelve. And something about your poor sister—heaven help us! And a sketch of our career in Paris, as they call it, and the way that we have got on and our great pretensions. And a passage about Blanche de Douves, Raoul's sister, who had that disease—what do they call it?—that she used to steal things in shops: do you see them reading that? And how did he know such a thing? it's ages ago—it's dead and buried!'

'You told me, you told me yourself,' said Francie, quickly. She turned red the instant she had spoken.

'Don't say it's you—don't, don't, my darling!' cried Mme de Brécourt, who had stared at her a moment. 'That's what I want, that's what you must do, that's what I see you this way for, first, alone. I've answered for you, you know; you must repudiate every responsibility. Margot suspects you—she has got that idea—she has given it to the others. I have told them they ought to be ashamed, that it's an outrage to you. I have done everything, for the last hour, to protect you. I'm your godmother, you know, and you mustn't disappoint me.

You're incapable, and you must say so, face to face, to my father. Think of Gaston, chérie, *he* will have seen it over there, alone, far from us all. Think of *his* horror and of *his* faith, of what *he* would expect of you.' Mme de Brécourt hurried on, and her companion's bewilderment deepened on seeing that the tears had risen to her eyes and were pouring down her cheeks. 'You must say to my father, face to face, that you are incapable—you are stainless.'

'Stainless?' Francie repeated. 'Of course I knew he wanted to write a piece about the picture and about my marriage.'

'About your marriage—of course you knew. Then wretched girl, you are at the bottom of *all*!' wailed Mme de Brécourt, flinging herself away from her, falling back on the sofa, covering her face with her hands.

'He told me—he told me when I went with him to the studio!' Francie declared, passionately. 'But he has printed more.'

'*More?* I should think so!' And Mme de Brecourt sprang up, standing before her. 'And you *let* him—about yourself? You gave him facts?'

'I told him—I told him—I don't know what. It was for his paper—he wants everything. It's a very fine paper.'

'A very fine paper?' Mme de Brécourt stared, with parted lips. 'Have you *seen*, have you touched the hideous sheet? Ah, my brother, my brother!' she wailed again, turning away.

'If your brother were here you wouldn't talk to me this way—he would protect me!' cried Francie, on her feet, seizing her little muff and moving to the door.

'Go away, go away or they'll kill you!' Mme de Brécourt went on, excitedly. 'After all I have done for you— after the way I have lied for you!' And she sobbed, trying to repress her sobs.

Francie, at this, broke out into a torrent of tears. 'I'll go home. Father, father!' she almost shrieked, reaching the door.

'Oh, your father—he has been a nice father, bringing you up in such ideas!' These words followed her with infinite scorn, but almost as Mme de Brécourt uttered them, struck by a sound, she sprang after the girl, seized her, drew her back and held her a moment, listening, before she could pass out. 'Hush—hush—they are coming in here, they are too anxious! Deny—deny it—say you know nothing! Your sister must have said things— and such things: say it all comes from *her*!'

'Oh, you dreadful—is that what *you* do?' cried Francie, shaking herself free. The door opened as she spoke and Mme de Brécourt walked quickly to the window, turning her back. Mme de Cliché was there and Mr Probert and M. de Brécourt and M. de Cliché. They entered in silence and M. de Brécourt, coming last, closed the door softly behind him. Francie had never been in a court of justice, but if she had had that experience these four persons would have reminded her of the jury filing back into their box with their verdict. They all looked at her hard as she stood in the middle of the room; Mme de Brécourt gazed out of the window, wiping her eyes; Mme de Cliché grasped a newspaper, crumpled and partly folded. Francie got a quick impression, moving her eyes from one face to another, that old Mr Probert was the worst; his mild ravaged expression was terrible. He was the one who looked at her least; he went to the fireplace and leaned on the mantel, with his head in his hands. He seemed ten years older.

'Ah, mademoiselle, mademoiselle, mademoiselle!' said Maxime de Cliché, slowly, impressively, in a tone of the most respectful but most poignant reproach.

'Have you seen it—have they sent it to you?' his wife asked, thrusting the paper towards her. 'It's quite at your service!' But as Francie neither spoke nor took it she tossed it upon the sofa, where, as it opened, falling, the girl read the name of the *Reverberator*. Mme de Cliché carried her head very far back.

'She has nothing to do with it—it's just as I told you— she's overwhelmed,' said Mme de Brécourt, remaining at the window.

'You would do well to read it—it's worth the trouble,' Alphonse de Brécourt remarked, going over to his wife. Francie saw him kiss her as he perceived her tears. She was angry at her own; she choked and swallowed them; they seemed somehow to put her in the wrong.

'Have you had no idea that any such monstrosity would be perpetrated?' Mme de Cliché went on, coming nearer to her. She had a manner of forced calmness—as if she wished it to be understood that she was one of those who could be reasonable under any provocation, though she were trembling within—which made Francie draw back. '*C'est pourtant rempli de choses*—which we know you to have been told of—by what folly, great heaven! It's right and left—no one is spared—it's a deluge of insult. My sister perhaps will have told you of the apprehensions I had—I couldn't resist them, though I thought of nothing so awful as this, God knows, the day I met you at Mr Waterlow's with your journalist.'

'I have told her everything—don't you see she's *anéantie*? Let her go, let her go!' exclaimed Mme de Brécourt, still at the window.

'Ah, your journalist, your journalist, mademoiselle!' said Maxime de Cliché. 'I am very sorry to have to say anything in regard to any friend of yours that can give you so little pleasure; but I promise myself the satisfaction of administering him with these hands a dressing he won't forget, if I may trouble you so far as to ask you to let him know it!'

M. de Cliché fingered the points of his moustache; he diffused some powerful scent; his eyes were dreadful to Francie. She wished Mr Probert would say something kind to her; but she had now determined to be strong. They were ever so many against one; Gaston was far away and she felt heroic. 'If you mean Mr Flack—I don't know what you mean,' she said as composedly as possible to M. de Cliché. 'Mr Flack has gone to London.'

At this M. de Brécourt gave a free laugh and his

brother-in-law replied, 'Ah, it's easy to go to London.'

'They like such things there; they do them more and more. It's as bad as America!' Mme de Cliché declared.

'Why have you sent for me—what do you all want me to do? You might explain—I am only an American girl!' said Francie, whose being only an American girl did not prevent her pretty head from holding itself now as high as Mme de Cliché's.

Mme de Brécourt came back to her quickly, laying her hand on her arm. 'You are very nervous—you had much better go home. I will explain everything to them—I will make them understand. The carriage is here—it had orders to wait.'

'I'm not in the least nervous, but I have made you all so,' Francie replied, laughing.

'I defend you, my dear young lady—I insist that you are only a wretched victim, like ourselves,' M. de Brécourt remarked, approaching her with a smile. 'I see the hand of a woman in it, you know,' he went on to the others; 'for there are strokes of a vulgarity that a man doesn't sink to (he can't, his very organisation prevents him) even if he be the greatest cad on earth. But please don't doubt that I have maintained that that woman is not you.'

'The way you talk—I don't know how to write,' said Francie.

'My poor child, when one knows you as I do!' murmured Mme de Brécourt, with her arm around her.

'There's a lady who helps him—Mr Flack has told me

so,' Francie continued. 'She's a literary lady—here in Paris—she writes what he tells her. I think her name is Miss Topping, but she calls herself Florine—or Dorine,' Francie added.

'Miss Dosson, you're too rare!' Marguerite de Cliché exclaimed, giving a long moan of pain which ended in an incongruous laugh. 'Then you have been three to it,' she went on; 'that accounts for its perfection!'

Francie disengaged herself again from Mme de Brécourt and went to Mr Probert, who stood looking down at the fire, with his back to her. 'Mr Probert, I'm very sorry at what I've done to distress you; I had no idea you would all feel so badly. I didn't mean any harm. I thought you would like it.'

The old man turned a little, bending his eyes on her, but without taking her hand as she had hoped. Usually when they met he kissed her. He did not look angry but he looked very ill. A strange inarticulate sound, a kind of exclamation of amazement and mirth, came from the others when she said she thought they would like it; and indeed poor Francie was far from being able to judge of the droll effect of that speech. 'Like it—*like it?*' said Mr Probert, staring at her as if he were a little afraid of her.

'What do you mean? She admits—she admits!' cried Mme de Cliché to her sister. 'Did you arrange it all that day in the Bois—to punish me for having tried to separate you?' she pursued, to the girl, who stood gazing up piteously at the old man.

'I don't know what he has published—I haven't seen

144

it—I don't understand. I thought it was only to be a piece about me.'

'About me!' M. de Cliché repeated in English. '*Elle est divine!*' He turned away, raising his shoulders and hands and then letting them fall.

Mme de Brécourt had picked up the newspaper; she rolled it together, saying to Francie that she must take it home, take it home immediately—then she would see. She only seemed to wish to get her out of the room. But Mr Probert had fixed the girl with his sick stare. 'You gave information for that? You desired it?'

'Why, I didn't desire it, but Mr Flack did.'

'Why do you know such ruffians? Where was your father?' the old man groaned.

'I thought he would just praise my picture and give pleasure to Mr Waterlow,' Francie went on. 'I thought he would just speak about my being engaged and give a little account; so many people in America would be interested.'

'So many people in America—that's just the dreadful thought, my dear,' said Mme de Brécourt, kindly. '*Voyons*, put it in your muff and tell us what you think of it.' And she continued to thrust forward the scandalous journal.

But Francie took no notice of it; she looked round from Mr Probert at the others. 'I told Gaston I should do something you wouldn't like.'

'Well, he'll believe it now!' cried Mme de Cliché.

'My poor child, do you think he will like it any better?' asked Mme de Brécourt.

Francie fastened her eyes on her a moment. 'He'll see it over there—he has seen it now.'

'Oh, my dear, you'll have news of him. Don't be afraid!' laughed Mme de Cliché.

'Did *he* send you the paper?' the girl went on, to Mr Probert.

'It was not directed in his hand,' said M. de Brécourt. 'There was some stamp on the band—it came from the office.'

'Mr Flack—is that his hideous name?—must have seen to that,' Mme de Brécourt suggested.

'Or perhaps Florine,' M. de Cliché interposed. 'I should like to get hold of Florine.'

'I did—I did tell him so!' Francie repeated, with her innocent face, alluding to her statement of a moment before and speaking as if she thought the circumstance detracted from the offence.

'So did I—so did we all!' said Mme de Cliché.

'And will he suffer—as you suffer?' Francie continued, appealing to Mr Probert.

'Suffer, suffer? He'll die!' cried the old man. 'However, I won't answer for him; he'll tell you himself, when he returns.'

'He'll die?' asked Francie, with expanded eyes.

'He'll never return—how can he show himself?' said Mme de Cliché.

'That's not true—he'll come back to stand by me!' the girl flashed out.

'How could you not feel that we were the last—the

very last?' asked Mr Probert, very gently. 'How could you not feel that my son was the very last—?'

'*C'est un sens qui lui manque!*' commented Mme de Cliché.

'Let her go, papa—do let her go home,' Mme de Brécourt pleaded.

'Surely. That's the only place for her to-day,' the elder sister continued.

'Yes, my child—you oughtn't to be here. It's your father—he ought to understand,' said Mr Probert.

'For God's sake don't send for him—let it all stop!' Mme de Cliché exclaimed.

Francie looked at her; then she said, 'Good-bye, Mr Probert—good-bye, Susan.'

'Give her your arm—take her to the carriage,' she heard Mme de Brécourt say to her husband. She got to the door she hardly knew how—she was only conscious that Susan held her once more long enough to kiss her. Poor Susan wanted to comfort her; that showed how bad (feeling as she did) she believed the whole business would yet be. It would be bad because Gaston—Gaston: Francie did not complete that thought, yet only Gaston was in her mind as she hurried to the carriage. M. de Brécourt hurried beside her; she would not take his arm. But he opened the door for her and as she got in she heard him murmur strangely, 'You are charming, mademoiselle—charming, charming!'

XII

HER absence had not been long and when she re-entered the familiar salon at the hotel she found her father and sister sitting there together as if they were timing her—a prey to curiosity and suspense. Mr Dosson however gave no sign of impatience; he only looked at her in silence through the smoke of his cigar (he profaned the red-satin splendour with perpetual fumes) as she burst into the room. No other word than the one I use expresses the tell-tale character of poor Francie's ingress. She rushed to one of the tables, flinging down her muff and gloves, and the next moment Delia, who had sprung up as she came in, had caught her in her arms and was glaring into her face with a 'Francie Dosson—what *have* you been through?' Francie said nothing at first, only closing her eyes and letting her sister do what she would with her. 'She has been crying, father—she *has*,' Delia went on, pulling her down upon a sofa and almost shaking her as she continued. 'Will you please tell? I've been perfectly wild! Yes you have, you dreadful—!' the elder girl declared, kissing her on the eyes. They opened at this compassionate pressure and Francie rested them in their beautiful distress on her father, who had now risen to his feet and stood with his back to the fire.

'Why, daughter,' said Mr Dosson, 'you look as if you had had quite a worry.'

'I told you I should—I told you, I told you!' Francie

broke out, with a trembling voice. 'And now it's come!'

'You don't mean to say you've *done* anything?' cried Delia, very white.

'It's all over—it's all over!' Francie pursued, turning her eyes to her sister.

'Are you crazy, Francie?' this young lady asked. 'I'm sure you look as if you were.'

'Ain't you going to be married, my child?' asked Mr Dosson, benevolently, coming nearer to her.

Francie sprang up, releasing herself from her sister, and threw her arms around him. 'Will you take me away, father—will you take me right away?'

'Of course I will, my precious. I'll take you anywhere. I don't want anything—it wasn't *my* idea!' And Mr Dosson and Delia looked at each other while the girl pressed her face upon his shoulder.

'I never heard such trash—you can't behave that way! Has he got engaged to someone else—in America?' Delia demanded.

'Why, if it's over it's over. I guess it's all right,' said Mr Dosson, kissing his younger daughter. 'I'll go back or I'll go on. I'll go anywhere you like.'

'You won't have your daughters insulted, I presume!' Delia cried. 'If you don't tell me this moment what has happened I'll drive straight round there and find out.'

'*Have* they insulted you, sweetie?' asked the old man, bending over the girl, who simply leaned upon him with her hidden face, with no sound of tears.

Francie raised her head, turning round upon her

sister. 'Did I ever tell you anything else—did I ever believe in it for an hour?'

'Oh, well, if you've done it on purpose—to triumph over me—we might as well go home, certainly. But I think you had better wait till Gaston comes.'

'It will be worse when he comes—if he thinks the same as they do.'

'*Have* they insulted you—have they?' Mr Dosson repeated; while the smoke of his cigar, curling round the question, gave him the air of asking it with placidity.

'They think I've insulted them—they're in an awful state—they're almost dead. Mr Flack has put it into the paper—everything, I don't know what—and they think it's too fearful. They were all there together—all at me at once, groaning and carrying on. I never saw people so affected.'

Delia listened in bewilderment, staring. 'So affected?'

'Ah, yes, there's a good deal of that,' said Mr Dosson.

'It's too real—too terrible; you don't understand. It's all printed there—that they're immoral, and everything about them; everything that's private and dreadful.'

'Immoral, is that so?' Mr Dosson asked.

'And about me, too, and about Gaston and my marriage, and all sorts of personalities, and all the names, and Mme de Villepreux, and everything. It's all printed there and they've read it. It says that one of them steals.'

'Will you be so good as to tell me what you are talking about?' Delia inquired, sternly. 'Where is it printed and what have we got to do with it?'

'Someone sent it, and I told Mr Flack.'

'Do you mean *his* paper? Oh the horrid brute!' Delia cried, with passion.

'Do they mind so what they see in the papers?' asked Mr Dosson. 'I guess they haven't seen what I've seen. Why, there used to be things about me——!'

'Well, it *is* about us too, about every one. They think it's the same as if I wrote it.'

'Well, you know what you *could* do,' said Mr Dosson, smiling at his daughter.

'Do you mean that piece about your picture—that you told me about when you went with him again to see it?' Delia asked.

'Oh, I don't know what piece it is; I haven't seen it.'

'Haven't seen it? Didn't they show it to you?'

'Yes, but I couldn't read it. Mme de Brécourt wanted me to take it—but I left it behind.'

'Well, that's like you—like the Tauchnitzes littering up our track. I'll be bound I'd see it,' said Delia. 'Hasn't it come, doesn't it always come?'

'I guess we haven't had the last—unless it's somewhere round,' said Mr Dosson.

'Father, go out and get it—you can buy it on the boulevard!' Delia continued. 'Francie, what *did* you want to tell him?'

'I didn't know; I was just conversing; he seemed to take so much interest.'

'Oh, he's a deep one!' groaned Delia.

'Well, if folks are immoral you can't keep it out of the

papers—and I don't know as you ought to want to,' Mr Dosson remarked. 'If they are I'm glad to know it, lovey.' And he gave his younger daughter a glance apparently intended to show that in this case he should know what to do.

But Francie was looking at her sister as if her attention had been arrested. 'How do you mean—"a deep one"?'

'Why, he wanted to break it off, the wretch!'

Francie stared; then a deeper flush leapt to her face, in which already there was a look of fever. 'To break off my engagement?'

'Yes, just that. But I'll be hanged if he shall. Father, will you allow that?'

'Allow what?'

'Why Mr Flack's vile interference. You won't let him do as he likes with us, I suppose, will you?'

'It's all done—it's all done!' said Francie. The tears had suddenly started into her eyes again.

'Well, he's so smart that it *is* likely he's too smart,' said Mr Dosson. 'But what did they want you to do about it?—that's what I want to know?'

'They wanted me to say I knew nothing about it—but I couldn't.'

'But you didn't and you don't—if you haven't even read it!' Delia returned.

'Where *is* the d—d thing?' her father asked, looking helplessly about him.

'On the boulevard, at the very first of those kiosks

you come to. That old woman has it—the one who speaks English—she always has it. Do go and get it—*do!*' And Delia pushed him, looked for his hat for him.

'I knew he wanted to print something and I can't say I didn't!' Francie said. 'I thought he would praise my portrait and that Mr Waterlow would like that, and Gaston and every one. And he talked to me about the paper—he is always doing that and always was—and I didn't see the harm. But even just knowing him—they think that's vile.'

'Well, I should hope we can know whom we like!' Delia declared, jumping in her mystification and alarm from one point of view to another.

Mr Dosson had put on his hat—he was going out for the paper. 'Why, he kept us alive last year,' he said.

'Well, he seems to have killed us now,' Delia cried.

'Well, don't give up an old friend,' said Mr Dosson, with his hand on the door. 'And don't back down on anything you've done.'

'Lord, what a fuss about an old newspaper!' Delia went on, in her exasperation. 'It must be about two weeks old, anyway. Didn't they ever see a society-paper before?'

'They can't have seen much,' said Mr Dosson. He paused, still with his hand on the door. 'Don't you worry —Gaston will make it all right.'

'Gaston?—it will kill Gaston!'

'Is that what they say?' Delia demanded.

'Gaston will never look at me again.'

'Well, then, he'll have to look at *me*,' said Mr Dosson.

'Do you mean that he'll give you up—that he'll be so abject?' Delia went on.

'They say he's just the one who will feel it most. But I'm the one who does that,' said Francie, with a strange smile.

'They're stuffing you with lies—because *they* don't like it. He'll be tender and true,' answered Delia.

'When *they* hate me?—Never!' And Francie shook her head slowly, still with her touching smile. 'That's what he cared for most—to make them like me.'

'And isn't he a gentleman, I should like to know?' asked Delia.

'Yes, and that's why I won't marry him—if I've injured him.'

'Pshaw! he has seen the papers over there. You wait till he comes,' Mr Dosson enjoined, passing out of the room.

The girls remained there together and after a moment Delia exclaimed: 'Well, he has got to fix it—that's one thing I can tell you.'

'Who has got to fix it?'

'Why, that villainous man. He has got to publish another piece saying it's all false or all a mistake.'

'Yes, you had better make him,' said Francie, with a weak laugh. 'You had better go after him—down to Nice.'

'You don't mean to say he has gone to Nice?'

'Didn't he say he was going there as soon as he came

back from London—going right through, without stopping?'

'I don't know but he did,' said Delia. Then she added —'The coward!'

'Why do you say that? He can't hide at Nice—they can find him there.'

'Are they going after him?'

'They want to shoot him—to stab him, I don't know what—those men.'

'Well, I wish they would,' said Delia.

'They had better shoot me. I shall defend him. I shall protect him,' Francie went on.

'How can you protect him? You shall never speak to him again.'

Francie was silent a moment. 'I can protect him without speaking to him. I can tell the simple truth—that he didn't print a word but what I told him.'

'That can't be so. He fixed it up. They always do, in the papers. Well now, he has got to bring out a piece praising them up—praising them to the skies: that's what he has got to do!' Delia declared, with decision.

'Praising them up? They'll hate that worse,' Francie returned, musingly.

Delia stared. 'What on earth do they want then?'

Francie had sunk upon the sofa; her eyes were fixed on the carpet. She made no reply to her sister's question but presently she said, 'We had better go to-morrow, the first hour that's possible.'

'Go where? Do you mean to Nice?'

'I don't care where. Anywhere, to get away.'

'Before Gaston comes—without seeing him?'

'I don't want to see him. When they were all ranting and raving at me just now I wished he was there—I told them so. But now I feel differently—I can never see him again.'

'I don't suppose you are crazy, are you?' cried Delia.

'I can't tell him it wasn't me—I can't, I can't!' the younger girl pursued.

Delia planted herself in front of her. 'Francie Dosson, if you're going to tell him you've done anything wrong you might as well stop before you begin. Didn't you hear what father said?'

'I'm sure I don't know,' Francie replied, listlessly.

' "Don't give up an old friend—there's nothing on earth so mean." Now isn't Gaston Probert an old friend?'

'It will be very simple—he will give me up.'

'Then he'll be a low wretch.'

'Not in the least—he'll give me up as he took me. He would never have asked me to marry him if he hadn't been able to get *them* to accept me: he thinks everything in life of *them*. If they cast me off now he'll do just the same. He'll have to choose between us, and when it comes to that he'll never choose me.'

'He'll never choose Mr Flack, if that's what you mean —if you are going to identify yourself so with *him*!'

'Oh, I wish he'd never been born!' Francie suddenly shivered. And then she added that she was sick—she was going to bed, and her sister took her off to her room.

Mr Dosson, that afternoon, sitting by Francie's bed-
side, read out from the copy of the *Reverberator* which he
had purchased on the boulevard the dreadful 'piece' to
his two daughters. It is a remarkable fact that as a family
they were rather disappointed in this composition, in
which their curiosity found less to repay it than it had
expected, their resentment against Mr Flack less to stimu-
late it, their imaginative effort to take the point of view
of the Proberts less to sustain it, and their acceptance of
the promulgation of Francie's innocent remarks as a
natural incident of the life of the day less to make them
reconsider it. The letter from Paris appeared lively,
'chatty,' even brilliant, and so far as the personalities
contained in it were concerned Mr Dosson wanted to
know if they were not aware over here of the charges
brought every day against the most prominent men in
Boston. 'If there was anything in that style they might
talk,' he said, and he scanned the effusion afresh with a
certain surprise at not finding in it some imputation of
pecuniary malversation. The effect of an acquaintance
with the text was to depress Delia, who did not exactly
see what there was in it to take back or explain away.
However, she was aware there were some points they
didn't understand, and doubtless these were the scandalous places—the things that had thrown the Proberts
into a state. But why should they be in a state if other
people didn't understand the allusions—they were peculiar, but peculiarly incomprehensible—any better than
she did? The whole thing struck Francie as infinitely less

lurid than Mme de Brécourt's account of it, and the part
about herself and her portrait seemed to make even less
of the subject than it easily might have done. It was
scanty, it was 'skimpy', and if Mr Waterlow was offended
it would not be because they had published too much
about him. It was nevertheless clear to her that there were
a lot of things *she* had not told Mr Flack, as well as a
great many that she had: perhaps these were the things
that that lady had put in—Florine or Dorine—the one
she had mentioned at Mme de Brécourt's.

All the same, if the communication in the *Reverberator*
gave them at the hotel less of a sensation than had been
announced and bristled so much less than was to have
been feared with explanations of the anguish of the Proberts, this did not diminish the girl's sense of responsibility nor make the case a whit less grave. It only showed
how sensitive and fastidious the Proberts were and therefore with what difficulty they could forgive. Moreover
Francie made another reflection as she lay there—for
Delia kept her in bed nearly three days, feeling that for
the moment at any rate that was an effectual reply to the
wish she had signified that they should leave Paris. Perhaps they had got coarse and callous, Francie said to herself; perhaps they had read so many articles like that that
they had lost their delicacy, the sense of certain differences
and decencies. Then, very weak and vague and passive
as she was now, in the bedimmed room, in the soft
Parisian bed, and with Delia treating her as much as
possible like a sick person, she thought of the lively and

chatty letters that they had always seen in the papers and wondered whether they *all* meant a violation of sanctities, a convulsion of homes, a burning of smitten faces, a rupture of girls' engagements. It was present to her as an agreeable negative, I must add, that her father and sister took no strenuous view of her responsibility or of their own: they neither brought the matter up to her as a crime nor made her worse through her feeling that they hovered about in tacit disapproval. There was a pleasant, cheerful helplessness in her father in regard to this as in regard to everything else. There could be no more discussion among them on such a question than there had ever been, for none was needed to illustrate the fact that for these candid minds the newspapers and all they contained were a part of the general fatality of things, of the recurrent freshness of the universe, coming out like the sun in the morning or the stars at night. The thing that worried Francie most while Delia kept her in bed was the apprehension of what her father might do: but this was not a fear of what he might do to Mr Flack. He would go round perhaps to Mr Probert's or to Mme de Brécourt's to reprimand them for having made things so rough for his 'chicken'. It was true she had scarcely ever seen him reprimand anyone for anything; but on the other hand nothing like that had ever happened before to her or to Delia. They had made each other cry once or twice but no one else had ever made them, and no one had ever broken out on them that way and frightened them half to death. Francie wanted her father not to go

round; she had a sense that those other people had somehow stores of censure, of superiority in any discussion,
which he could not command. She wanted nothing done
and no communication to pass—only a proud, unbicker-
ing silence on the part of the Dossons. If the Proberts
made a noise and they made none it would be they who
would have the best appearance. Moreover, now, with
each elapsing day she felt that she *did* wish to see Gaston
about it. Her desire was to wait, counting the hours, so
that she might just explain, saying two or three things.
Perhaps these things would not make it better—very
likely they would not; but at any rate nothing would
have been done in the interval, at least on her part and
her father's and Delia's, to make it worse. She told her
father that she should not like him to go round, and she
was in some degree relieved at perceiving that he did not
seem very clear as to what it was open to him to say to
the Proberts. He was not afraid but he was vague. His
relation to almost everything that had happened to them
as a family for a good while back was a sense of the
absence of precedents, and precedents were particularly
absent now, for he had never before seen a lot of people
in a rage about a piece in the paper. Delia also reassured
her; she said she would see to it that their father didn't
dash off. She communicated to her indeed that he had not
the smallest doubt that Gaston, in a few days, would
blow them all up much higher than they had blown her
and that he was very sorry he had let her go round on
that sort of summons to Mme de Brécourt's. It was for

her and the rest to come to Francie and to him, and if
they had anything practical to say they would arrive in
a body yet. If Mr Dosson had the sense of his daughter's
having been roughly handled he derived some of the
consolation of amusement from his persistent humorous
view of the Proberts as a 'body'. If they were consistent
with their character or with their complaint they would
move *en masse* upon the hotel, and he stayed at home a
good deal, as if he were waiting for them. Delia intimated
to her sister that this vision cheered them up as they sat,
they two, in the red salon while Francie was in bed. Of
course it did not exhilarate this young lady, and she even
looked for no brighter side now. She knew almost nothing but her sharp little ache of suspense, her presentiment
of Gaston's horror, which grew all the while. Delia remarked to her once that he would have seen lots of
society-papers over there, he would have become familiar;
but this only suggested to the girl (she had strange new
moments of quick reasoning at present,) that that really
would only prepare him to be disgusted, not to be indifferent. His disgust would be colder than anything she
had ever known and would complete her knowledge of
him—make her understand him properly for the first
time. She would just meet it as briefly as possible; it
would finish the business, wind up the episode, and all
would be over.

He did not write; that proved it in advance; there
had now been two or three posts without a letter. He had
seen the paper in Boston or in New York and it had

struck him dumb. It was very well for Delia to say that of course he didn't write when he was on the sea: how could they get his letters even if he did? There had been time before—before he sailed; though Delia represented that people never wrote then. They were ever so much too busy at the last and they were going to see their correspondents in a few days anyway. The only missives that came to Francie were a copy of the *Reverberator*, addressed in Mr Flack's hand and with a great inkmark on the margin of the fatal letter, and a long note from Mme de Brécourt, received forty-eight hours after the scene at her house. This lady expressed herself as follows:

'My DEAR FRANCIE,—I felt very badly after you had gone yesterday morning, and I had twenty minds to go and see you. But we have talked it over conscientiously and it appears to us that we have no right to take any such step till Gaston arrives. The situation is not exclusively ours but belongs to him as well, and we feel that we ought to make it over to him in as simple and compact a form as possible. Therefore, as we regard it, we had better not touch it (it's so delicate, isn't it, my poor child?) but leave it just as it is. They think I even exceed my powers in writing you these simple lines, and that once your participation has been *constatée* (which was the only advantage of that dreadful scene), *everything* should stop. But I have liked you, Francie, I have believed in you, and I don't wish you to be able to say that in spite of the thunderbolt you have drawn down upon us I have not treated you with tenderness. It is a thunderbolt indeed, my poor and innocent but disastrous little friend! We are hearing more of it already— the horrible Republican papers here have (*as we know*) already got hold of the unspeakable sheet and are preparing to reproduce the article: that is such parts of it as they may put forward (with innuendoes and *sous-entendus* to eke out the rest) without exposing themselves to a suit for defamation. Poor Léonie de Villepreux has been with us constantly and Jeanne and her husband have telegraphed that we may expect them day after to-morrow. They are evidently immensely *émotionnés*, for they almost never telegraph. They wish so to receive Gaston. We have determined all the same to be intensely *quiet*, and that will be sure to be his view. Alphonse and Maxime now recognise that it is best to leave Mr Flack alone, hard as it is to keep one's hands off him. Have you anything to *lui faire dire*—to my precious brother when he arrives? But it is foolish of me to ask you that, for you had much better not answer this. You will no doubt have an opportunity to say to him—whatever, my dear Francie, you *can* say! It will matter comparatively little that you may never be able to say it to your friend, with every allowance,

'SUZANNE DE BRÉCOURT.'

Francie looked at this letter and tossed it away without reading it. Delia picked it up, read it to her father, who didn't understand it, and kept it in her possession, poring over it as Mr Flack had seen her pore over the cards that were left while she was out or over the registers of American travellers. They knew of Gaston's arrival by his telegraphing from Havre (he came back by the French line), and he mentioned the hour—'about dinner-time'—at which he should reach Paris. Delia, after dinner, made her father take her to the circus, so that Francie should be left alone to receive her intended, who would be sure to hurry round in the course of the evening. The girl herself expressed no preference whatever on this point, and the idea was one of Delia's masterly ones, her flashes of inspiration. There was never any difficulty about imposing such conceptions on her father. But at half-past ten, when they returned, the young man had not appeared, and Francie remained only long enough to say, 'I told you so!' with a white face and to march off to her room with her candle. She locked herself in and her sister could not get at her that night. It was another of Delia's inspirations not to try, after she had felt that the door was fast. She forbore, in the exercise of a great discretion, but she herself in the ensuing hours slept not a wink. Nevertheless, the next morning, as early as ten o'clock, she had the energy to drag her father out to the banker's and to keep him out two hours. It would be inconceivable now that Gaston should not turn up before the *déjeuner*. He did turn up; about eleven o'clock he came in and found Francie alone. She perceived in the strangest way, that he was very pale, at the same time that he was sunburnt; and not for an instant did he smile at her. It was very certain that there was no bright flicker in her own face, and they had the most singular, the most unnatural meeting. As he entered the room he said— 'I could not come last evening; they made it impossible; they were all there and we were up till three o'clock this morning.' He looked as if he had been through terrible things, and it was not simply the strain of his attention to so much business in America. What passed next she could not remember afterwards; it seemed only a few seconds before he said to her, slowly, holding her hand (before this he had pressed his lips to hers silently), 'Is it true, Francie, what they say (and they swear to it!) that *you* told that blackguard those horrors—that that infamous letter is only a report of *your* talk?'

'I told him everything—it's all me, *me, Me!*' the girl replied, exaltedly, without pretending to hesitate an instant as to what he might mean.

Gaston looked at her with deep eyes; then he walked straight away to the window and remained there in silence. Francie said nothing more. At last the young man went on, 'And I who insisted to them that there was no natural delicacy like yours!'

'Well, you'll never need to insist about anything any more!' she cried. And with this she dashed out of the room by the nearest door. When Delia and Mr Dosson returned the red salon was empty and Francie was again locked in her room. But this time her sister forced an entrance.

XIII

Mr Dosson, as we know, was meditative, and the present occasion could only minister to that side of his nature, especially as, so far at least as the observation of his daughters went, it had not urged him into uncontrollable movement. But the truth is that the intensity, or rather the continuity, of his meditations did engender an act which was not perceived by these young ladies, though its consequences presently became definite enough. While he waited for the Proberts to arrive in a phalanx and noted that they failed to do so he had plenty of time to ask himself—and also to ask Delia—questions about Mr Flack. So far as they were addressed to his daughter they were promptly answered, for Delia had been ready from the first, as we have seen, to pronounce upon the conduct of the young journalist. Her view of it was clearer every hour; there was a difference, however, in the course of action which she judged this view to demand. At first he was to be blown up for the mess he had got them into (profitless as the process might be and vain the satisfaction); he was to be visited with the harshest chastisement that the sense of violated confidence could inflict. Now he was simply to be dropped, to be cut, to be let alone to his dying day: the girl quickly recognised that this was a much more distinguished way of showing displeasure. It was in this manner that she characterised it in her frequent conversations with her father, if that can be called conversation which consisted of his serenely smoking while she poured forth arguments which combined both variety and repetition. The same cause will produce consequences the most diverse: a truth according to which the catastrophe that made Delia express freely the hope that she might never again see so much as the end of Mr Flack's nose had just the opposite effect upon her father. The one thing he wanted positively to do at present was to let his eyes travel over his young friend's whole person: it seemed to him that that would really make him feel better. If there had been a discussion about this the girl would have kept the field, for she had the advantage of being able to tell her reasons, whereas her father could not have put his into words. Delia had touched on her deepest conviction in saying to Francie that the correspondent of the *Reverberator* had played them that trick on purpose to get them into such trouble with the Proberts that he might see his own hopes bloom again under cover of their disaster. This had many of the appearances of a strained interpretation, but that did not prevent Delia from placing it before her father several times an hour. It mattered little that he should remark, in return, that he didn't see what good it could do Mr Flack that Francie—and he and Delia, for all he could guess—should be disgusted with him: to Mr Dosson's mind that was such a queer way of reasoning. Delia maintained that she understood perfectly, though she couldn't explain—and at any rate she didn't want the manoeuvring creature to come flying back from Nice. She didn't want him to know that there had been a scandal, that they had a grievance against him, that any one had so much as heard of his article or cared what he published or didn't publish: above all she didn't want him to know that the Proberts had cooled off. Mixed up with this high rigour on Miss Dosson's part was the oddest secret complacency of reflection that in consequence of what Mr Flack *had* published the great American community was in a position to know with what fine folks Francie and she were associated. She hoped that some of the people who used to call on them when they were 'off to-morrow' would take the lesson to heart.

While she glowed with this consolation as well as with the resentment for which it was required her father quietly addressed a few words, by letter , to George Flack. This communication was not of a minatory order; it expressed on the contrary the loose sociability which was the essence of Mr Dosson's nature. He wanted to see Mr Flack, to talk the whole thing over, and the desire to hold him to an account would play but a small part in the interview. It was much more definite to him that the soreness of the Proberts was a kind of unexpected insanity (so little did his experience match it), than that a newspaper-man had misbehaved in trying to turn out an attractive article. As the newspaper-man happened to be the person with whom he had most consorted for some time back he felt drawn to him in the presence of a new problem, and somehow it did not seem to Mr Dosson to disqualify him as a source of comfort that it was just he who had been the fountain of injury. The injury was a sort of emanation of the crazy Proberts. Moreover Mr Dosson could not dislike at such short notice a man who had smoked so many of his cigars, ordered so many of his dinners and helped him so loyally to spend his money: such acts constituted a bond, and when there was a bond people gave it a little jerk in time of trouble. His letter to Nice was the little jerk.

The morning after Francie had turned her back on Gaston and left him planted in the salon (he had remained ten minutes, to see if she would reappear, and then had marched out of the hotel), she received by the first post a letter from him, written the evening before. It conveyed his deep regret that their meeting in the morning should have been of so painful, so unnatural a character, and the hope that she did not consider as her strange behaviour had seemed to suggest, that *she* had anything to complain of. There was too much he wanted to say and above all too much he wanted to ask, for him to consent to the indefinite postponement of a necessary interview. There were explanations, assurances, *de part et d'autre*, with which it was manifestly impossible that either of them should dispense. He would therefore propose that she should see him, and not be wanting in patience to that end, on the following evening. He did not propose an earlier moment because his hands were terribly full at home. Frankly speaking, the state of things there was of the worst. Jane and her husband had just arrived and had made him a violent, an unexpected scene. Two of the French newspapers had got hold of the article and had given the most perfidious extracts. His father had not stirred out of the house, had not put his foot inside of a club, for more than a week. Marguerite and Maxime were immediately to start for England, for an indefinite stay. They couldn't face their life in Paris. For himself, he was in the breach, fighting hard and making, on her behalf, asseverations which it was impossible for him to believe, in spite of the dreadful defiant confession she had appeared to throw at him in the morning, that she would not virtually confirm. He would come in as soon after nine as possible; the morrow, up to that time, would be severe in the Cours la Reine, and he begged her in the meantime not to doubt of his perfect tenderness. So far from his distress having made it less he had never yet felt so much that she had, in his affection, a treasure of indulgence to draw upon.

A couple of hours after this letter arrived Francie lay on one of the satin sofas with her eyes closed and her hand clinched upon it in her pocket. Delia sat near her with a needle in her fingers, certain morsels of silk and ribbon in her lap, several pins in her mouth, and her attention wandering constantly from her work to her sister's face. The weather was now so completely vernal that Mr Dosson was able to sit in the court, and he had lately resumed this practice, in which he was presumably at the present moment absorbed. Delia had lowered her needle and was watching Francie, to see if she were not asleep—she had been perfectly still for so long—when her glance was drawn to the door, which she heard pushed open. Mr Flack stood there, looking from one to the other of the young ladies, as if to see which of them would be most agreeably surprised by his visit.

'I saw your father down stairs—he says it's all right,' said the journalist, advancing and smiling. 'He told me to come straight up—I had quite a talk with him.'

'All right—*all right*?' Delia Dosson repeated, springing up. 'Yes, indeed, I should say so.' Then she checked herself, asking in another manner: 'Is that so? father sent you up?' And then, in still another: 'Well, have you had a good time at Nice?'

'You'd better all come down and see. It's lovely down there. If you'll come down I'll go right back. I guess you want a change,' Mr Flack went on. He spoke to Delia but he looked at Francie, who showed she had not been asleep by the quick consciousness with which she raised

herself on her sofa. She gazed at the visitor with parted
lips, but she said nothing. He hesitated a moment, then
came toward her, smiling, with his hand out. His bright
eyes were brighter than ever, but they had an odd appearance of being smaller, like penetrating points. 'Your
father has told me all about it. Did you ever hear of
anything so ridiculous?'

'All about what?—all about what?' said Delia, whose
attempt to represent happy ignorance seemed likely to be
spoiled by an intromission of ferocity. She might succeed
in appearing ignorant, but she could scarcely succeed in
appearing happy Francie had risen to her feet and had
suffered Mr Flack to possess himself for a moment of her
hand, but neither of the girls had asked the young man to
sit down. 'I thought you were going to stay a month at
Nice?' Delia continued.

'Well, I was, but your father's letter started me up.'

'Father's letter?'

'He wrote me about the row—didn't you know it?
Then I broke. You didn't suppose I was going to stay
down there when there were such times up here.'

'Gracious!' Delia exclaimed.

'Is it pleasant at Nice? Is it very gay? Isn't it very hot
now?' Francie asked.

'Oh, it's all right. But I haven't come up here to talk
about Nice, have I?'

'Why not, if we want to?' Delia inquired.

Mr Flack looked at her for a moment very hard, in the
whites of the eyes; then he replied, turning back to her

sister: 'Anything *you* like, Miss Francie. With you one subject is as good as another. Can't we sit down? Can't we be comfortable?' he added.

'Comfortable? of course we can!' cried Delia, but she remained erect while Francie sank upon the sofa again and their companion took possession of the nearest chair.

'Do you remember what I told you once, that the people *will* have the plums?' George Flack asked of the younger girl.

She looked for an instant as if she were trying to recollect what he had told her; then she said, '*Did* father write to you?'

'Of course he did. That's why I'm here.'

'Poor father, sometimes he doesn't know *what* to do!' Delia remarked.

'He told me the *Reverberator* has made a sensation. I guessed that for myself, when I saw the way the papers here were after it. That thing will go the round, you'll see! What brought me was learning from him that they *have* got their backs up.'

'What on earth are you talking about?' cried Delia.

Mr Flack turned his eyes on hers in the same way as a moment before; Francie sat there serious, looking hard at the carpet. 'What game are you trying, Miss Delia? It ain't true *you* care what I wrote, is it?' he pursued, addressing himself again to Francie.

She raised her eyes. 'Did you write it yourself?'

'What do you care what he wrote—or what does any one care?' Delia broke in.

'It has done the paper more good than anything—every one is so interested,' said Mr Flack, in the tone of reasonable explanation. 'And you don't feel that you have anything to complain of, do you?' he added, to Francie, kindly.

'Do you mean because I told you?'

'Why, certainly. Didn't it all spring out of that lovely drive and that walk in the Bois that we had, when you took me to see your portrait? Didn't you understand that I wanted you to know that the public would appreciate a column or two about Mr Waterlow's new picture, and about you as the subject of it, and about your being engaged to a member of the *grand monde*, and about what was going on in the *grand monde*, which would naturally attract attention through that? Why, Miss Francie, you talked as if you did.'

'Did I talk a great deal?' asked Francie.

'Why, most freely—it was too lovely. Don't you remember when we sat there in the Bois?'

'Oh, rubbish!' Delia ejaculated.

'Yes, and Mme de Cliché passed.'

'And you told me she was scandalised. And we laughed—it struck us as idiotic. I said it was affected and pretentious. Your father tells me she is scandalised now—she and all the rest of them—at their names appearing in the *Reverberator*. I don't hesitate to declare that that's affected and pretentious too. It ain't genuine—and if it is it doesn't count. They pretend to be shocked because it looks exclusive, but in point of fact they like it first-rate.'

'Are you talking about that old piece in the paper? Mercy, wasn't that dead and buried days and days ago?' Delia ejaculated. She hovered there in a fever of irritation, fidgeted by the revelation that her father had summoned Mr Flack to Paris, which struck her almost like a treachery because it seemed to denote a plan. A plan, and an uncommunicated plan, on Mr Dosson's part was unnatural and alarming; and there was further provocation in his appearing to shirk the responsibility of it by not having come up, at such a moment, with Mr Flack. Delia was impatient to know what he wanted anyway. Did he want to slide back to a common, though active, young man? Did he want to put Mr Flack forward with a shallow extemporised optimism as a substitute for the alienated Gaston? If she had not been afraid that something still more complicating than anything that had happened yet might come to pass between her two companions in case of her leaving them together she would have darted down to the court to appease her conjectures, to challenge her father and tell him she should be very much obliged to him if he wouldn't meddle. She felt liberated however, the next moment, for something occurred that struck her as a quick indication of her sister's present emotion.

'Do you know the view I take of the matter, according to what your father has told me?' Mr Flack inquired. 'I don't mean that he suggested the interpretation, but my own knowledge of the world (as the world is constituted over here!) forces it upon my mind. They are

scandalised, they are horrified. They never heard anything so dreadful. Miss Francie, that ain't good enough!
They know what's in the papers every day of their lives
and they know how it got there. They are simply making
the thing a pretext to break—because they don't think
you're fashionable enough. They're delighted to strike a
pretext they can work, and they're all as merry together
round there as a lot of boys when school don't keep.
That's my view of the business.'

'Oh—how can you say such a thing?' drawled Francie,
with a tremor in her voice that struck her sister. Her eyes
met Delia's at the same moment, and this young woman's
heart bounded with the sense that she was safe. Mr Flack's
indelicacy attempted to prove too much (though Miss
Dosson had crude notions about the license of the press
she felt, even as an untutored woman, what a false step
he was now taking), and it seemed to her that Francie,
who was revolted (the way she looked at her, in horror,
showed that), could be trusted to check his advance.

'What does it matter what he says, my dear?' she
cried. 'Do make him drop the subject—he's talking very
wild. I'm going down to see what father means—I never
heard of anything so flat!' At the door she paused a
moment to add mutely, with a pressing glance, 'Now just
wipe him out—mind!' It was the same injunction she
had launched at her from afar that day, a year before, they
all dined at Saint-Germain, and she could remember how
effective it had been then. The next moment she flirted
out.

THE REVERBERATOR

As soon as she had gone Mr Flack moved nearer to Francie. 'Now look here, you are not going back on me, are you?'

'Going back on you—what do you mean?'

'Ain't we together in this thing? Surely we are.'

'Together—together?' Francie repeated, looking at him.

'Don't you remember what I said to you—in the clearest terms—before we went to Waterlow's, before our drive? I notified you that I should make use of the whole thing.'

'Oh, yes, I understood—it was all for that. I told them so. I never denied it.'

'You told them so?'

'When they were crying and going on. I told them I knew it—I told them I gave you the tip, as they say.'

She felt Mr Flack's eyes on her, strangely, as she spoke these words; then he was still nearer to her—he had taken her hand. 'Ah, you're too sweet!' She disengaged her hand and in the effort she sprang up; but he, rising too, seemed to press always nearer—she had a sense (it was disagreeable) that he was demonstrative—so that she retreated a little before him. 'They were all there roaring and raging, trying to make you believe you have outraged them?'

'All but young Mr Probert. Certainly they don't like it.'

'The cowards!' said George Flack. 'And where was young Mr Probert?'

'He was away—I've told you—in America.'

'Ah, yes, your father told me. But now he has come back doesn't he like it either?'

'I don't know, Mr Flack,' Francie replied, impatiently.

'Well, I do, then. He's a coward too—he'll do what his papa tells him—and the countess and the duchess and all the rest: he'll just back down—he'll give you up.'

'I can't talk to you about that,' said Francie.

'Why not? why is he such a sacred subject, when we *are* together? You can't alter that. It was too lovely, your standing up for me—your not denying me!'

'You put in things I never said. It seems to me it was very different,' the girl remarked.

'Everything *is* different when it's printed. What else would be the good of papers? Besides, it wasn't I; it was a lady who helps me here—you've heard me speak of her: Miss Topping. She wants so much to know you—she wants to talk with you.'

'And will she publish that?' Francie asked, gravely.

Mr Flack stared a moment. 'Lord, how they have worked on you! And do *you* think it's bad?'

'Do I think what's bad?'

'Why the letter we are talking about.'

'Well—I don't like it.'

'Do you think I was dishonourable?'

The girl made no answer to this, but after a moment she said, 'Why do you come here this way—why do you ask me such questions?'

He hesitated; then he broke out: 'Because I love you—don't you know that?'

'Oh, please don't!' she almost moaned, turning away.

'Why won't you understand it—why won't you understand the rest? Don't you see how it has worked round—the heartless brutes they've turned into, and the way *our* life—yours and mine—is bound to be the same? Don't you see the base way they treat you and that *I* only want to do anything in the world for you?'

Francie made no immediate response to this appeal, but after a moment she began: 'Why did you ask me so many questions that day?'

'Because I always ask questions—it's my business to ask them. Haven't you always seen me ask you and ask every one all I could? Don't you know they are the very foundation of my work? I thought you sympathised with my work so much—you used to tell me you did.'

'Well, I did,' said Francie.

'You put it in the past, I see. You don't then any more.'

If this remark was on her visitor's part the sign of a rare assurance the girl's gentleness was still unruffled by it. She hesitated, she even smiled; then she replied, 'Oh yes, I do—only not so much.'

'They *have* worked on you; but I should have thought they would have disgusted you. I don't care—even a little sympathy will do—whatever you've got left.' He paused, looking at her, but she remained silent; so he went on: 'There was no obligation for you to answer my questions—you might have shut me up, that day, with a word.'

'Really?' Francie asked, with all her sweet good faith in her face. 'I thought I had to—for fear I should appear ungrateful.'

'Ungrateful?'

'Why to you—after what you had done. Don't you remember that it was you that introduced us——?' And she paused, with a kind of weary delicacy.

'Not to those snobs that are screaming like frightened peacocks. I beg your pardon—I haven't *that* on my conscience.'

'Well, you introduced us to Mr Waterlow and he introduced us to—to his friends,' Francie explained, blushing, as if it were a fault, for the inexactness engendered by her magnanimity. 'That's why I thought I ought to tell you what you'd like.'

'Why, do you suppose if I'd known where that first visit of ours to Waterlow was going to bring you out I'd have taken you within fifty miles—— ' He stopped suddenly; then in another tone, 'Lord, there's no one like you! And you told them it was all *you?*'

'Never mind what I told them.'

'Miss Francie,' said George Flack, 'if you'll marry me I'll never ask a question again. I'll go into some other business.'

'Then you didn't do it on purpose?' Francie asked.

'On purpose?'

'To get me into a quarrel with them—so that I might be free again.'

'Well, of all the ideas——!' the young man exclaimed,

staring. 'Your mind never produced that—it was your sister's.'

'Wasn't it natural it should occur to me, since if, as you say, you would never consciously have been the means—'

'Ah, but I *was* the means!' Mr Flack interrupted. 'We must go, after all, by what *did* happen.'

'Well, I thanked you when I drove with you and let you draw me out. So we're square, aren't we?' The term Francie used was a colloquialism generally associated with levity, but her face, as she spoke, was none the less deeply serious—serious even to pain.

'We're square?' Mr Flack repeated.

'I don't think you ought to ask for anything more. Good-bye.'

'Good-bye? Never!' cried the young man.

He had an air of flushing with disappointment which really showed that he had come with a certain confidence of success.

Something in the way Francie repeated her 'Good-bye!' indicated that she perceived this and that in the vision of such a confidence there was little to please her. 'Do go away!' she broke out.

'Well, I'll come back very soon,' said Mr Flack, taking his hat.

'Please don't—I don't like it.' She had now contrived to put a wide space between them.

'Oh, you tormentress!' he groaned. He went toward the door, but before he reached it he turned round. 'Will you tell me this, anyway? *Are* you going to marry Mr Probert—after this?'

'Do you want to put that in the paper?'

'Of course I do—and say you said it!' Mr Flack held up his head.

They stood looking at each other across the large room. 'Well then—I ain't. There!'

'That's all right,' said Mr Flack, going out.

XIV

WHEN Gaston Probert came in that evening he was received by Mr Dosson and Delia, and when he asked where Francie was he was told by Delia that she would show herself half an hour later. Francie had instructed her sister that as Gaston would have, first of all, information to give their father about the business he had transacted in America he wouldn't care for a lot of women in the room. When Delia made this speech before Mr Dosson the old man protested that he was not in any hurry for the business; what he wanted to find out most was whether he had a good time—whether he liked it over there. Gaston might have liked it, but he did not look as if he had had a very good time. His face told of reverses, of suffering; and Delia declared to him that if she had not received his assurance to the contrary she would have believed he was right down sick. He confessed that he had been very sick at sea and was still feeling the effect of it, but insisted that there was nothing the matter with him now. He sat for some time with Mr Dosson and Delia, and never once alluded to the cloud that hung over their relations. The girl had schooled her father to reticence on this point, and the manner in which she had descended upon him in the morning, after Mr Flack had come up stairs, was a lesson he was not likely soon to forget. It had been impressed upon him that she was indeed wiser than he could pretend to be, and he was now mindful that he must not speak of the 'piece in the paper' unless young Probert should speak of it first. When Delia rushed down to him in the court she began by asking him categorically whom he had wished to do good to by sending Mr Flack up to their parlour. To Francie or to her? Why, the way they felt then, they detested his very name. To Mr Flack himself? Why, he had simply exposed him to the biggest snub he had ever got in his life.

'Well, hanged if I understand!' poor Mr Dosson had said. 'I thought you liked the piece—you think it's so queer *they* don't like it.' 'They,' in the parlance of the Dossons, now never meant anything but the Proberts in congress assembled.

'I don't think anything is queer but you!' Delia had retorted; and she had let her father know that she had left Francie in the very act of 'handling' Mr Flack.

'Is that so?' the old gentleman had asked, helplessly.

Francie's visitor came down a few minutes later and passed through the court and out of the hotel without looking at them. Mr Dosson had been going to call after him, but Delia checked him with a violent pinch. The unsociable manner of the young journalist's departure added to Mr Dosson's sense of the mystery of things. I think this may be said to have been the only incident in the whole business that gave him a personal pang. He remembered how many of his cigars he had smoked with Mr Flack, and how universal a participant he had made him. This struck him as the failure of friendship, and not the publication of details about the Proberts. Deep in Mr Dosson's spirit was a sense that if these people had done bad things they ought to be ashamed of themselves and he couldn't pity them, and if they hadn't done them there was no need of making such a rumpus about other people knowing. It was therefore, in spite of the young man's rough exit, still in the tone of American condonation that he had observed to Delia: 'He says that's what they like over there and that it stands to reason that if you start a paper you've got to give them what they like. If you want the people with you, you've got to be with the people.'

'Well, there are a good many people in the world. I don't think the Proberts are with us much.'

'Oh, he doesn't mean them,' said Mr Dosson.

'Well, I do!' cried Delia.

At one of the ormolu tables, near a lamp with a pink shade, Gaston insisted on making at least a partial statement. He did not say that he might never have another chance, but Delia felt with despair that this idea was in his mind. He was very gentle, very polite, but distinctly cold, she thought; he was intensely depressed and for half an hour uttered not the least little pleasantry. There was no particular occasion for that when he talked about 'preferred bonds' with her father. This was a language Delia could not translate, though she had heard it from childhood. He had a great many papers to show Mr Dosson, records of the mission of which he had acquitted himself, but Mr Dosson pushed them into the drawer of the ormolu table with the remark that he guessed they were all right. Now, after the fact, he appeared to attach but little importance to Gaston's achievements—an attitude which Delia perceived to be slightly disconcerting to the young man. Delia understood it: she had an instinctive sense that her father knew a great deal more than Gaston could tell him even about the work he had committed to him, and also that there was in such punctual settlements an eagerness, a literalism totally foreign to Mr Dosson's domestic habits. If Gaston had cooled off he wanted at least to be able to say that he had rendered them services in America; but now her father, for the moment at least, scarcely appeared to think his services worth speaking of: a circumstance that left him with more of the responsibility for his cooling. What Mr Dosson wanted to know was how everything had struck him over there, especially the Pickett Building and the parlour-cars and Niagara and the hotels he had instructed him to go to, giving him an introduction in two or three cases to the gentleman in charge of the office. It was in relation to these themes that Gaston was guilty of a want

of spring, as the girl phrased it to herself; that he evinced
no superficial joy. He declared however, repeatedly, that
it was a most extraordinary country—most extraordinary
and far beyond anything he had had any conception of.
'Of course I didn't like *everything*,' he said, 'any more
than I like everything anywhere.'

'Well, what didn't you like?' Mr Dosson genially inquired.

Gaston Probert hesitated. 'Well, the light for instance.'

'The light—the electric?'

'No, the solar! I thought it rather hard, too much like
the scratching of a slate-pencil.' As Mr Dosson looked
vague at this, as if the reference were to some enterprise
(a great lamp company) of which he had not heard—con-
veying a suggestion that he was perhaps staying away too
long, Gaston immediately added: 'I really think Francie
might come in. I wrote to her that I wanted particularly
to see her.'

'I will go and call her—I'll make her come,' said Delia,
going out. She left her companions together and Gaston
returned to the subject of Mr Munster, Mr Dosson's
former partner, to whom he had taken a letter and who
had showed him every sort of civility. Mr Dosson was
pleased at this; nevertheless he broke out, suddenly—

'Look here, you know; if you've got anything to say
that you don't think very acceptable you had better say
it to *me*.' Gaston coloured, but his reply was checked by
Delia's quick return. She announced that her sister would
be obliged if he would go into the little dining-room—

he would find her there. She had something to communicate to him that she could mention only in private. It was very comfortable; there was a lamp and a fire. 'Well, I guess she *can* take care of herself!' Mr Dosson, at this, commented, laughing. 'What does she want to say to him?' he demanded, when Gaston had passed out.

'Gracious knows! She won't tell me. But it's too flat, at his age, to live in such terror.'

'In such terror?'

'Why, of your father. You've got to choose.'

'How, to choose?'

'Why, if there's a person you like and he doesn't like.'

'You mean you can't choose your father,' said Mr Dosson, thoughtfully.

'Of course you can't.'

'Well then, please don't like any one. But perhaps *I* should like him,' added Mr Dosson, faithful to his cheerful tradition.

'I guess you'd have to,' said Delia.

In the small *salle-à-manger*, when Gaston went in, Francie was standing by the empty table, and as soon as she saw him she said—'You can't say I didn't tell you that I should do something. I did nothing else, from the first. So you were warned again and again; you knew what to expect.'

'Ah, don't say that again; if you knew how it acts on my nerves!' the young man groaned. 'You speak as if you had done it on purpose—to carry out your absurd threat.'

'Well, what does it matter, when it's all over?'

'It's not all over. Would to God it were!'

The girl stared. 'Don't you know what I sent for you to come in here for? To bid you good-bye.'

'Francie, what has got into you?' he said. 'What deviltry, what poison?' It would have been a singular sight to an observer, the opposition of these young figures, so fresh, so candid, so meant for confidence, but now standing apart and looking at each other in a wan defiance which hardened their faces.

'Don't they despise me—don't they hate me? You do yourself! Certainly you'll be glad for me to break off and spare you such a difficulty, such a responsibility.'

'I don't understand; it's like some hideous dream!' Gaston Probert cried. 'You act as if you were doing something for a wager, and you talk so. I don't believe it —I don't believe a word of it.'

'What don't you believe?'

'That you told him—that you told him knowingly. If you'll take that back (it's too monstrous!) if you'll deny it and declare you were practised upon and surprised, everything can still be arranged.'

'Do you want me to lie?' asked Francie Dosson. 'I thought you would like it.'

'Oh, Francie, Francie!' moaned the wretched youth, with tears in his eyes.

'What can be arranged? What do you mean by every thing?' she went on.

'Why, they'll accept it; they'll ask for nothing more. It's your participation they can't forgive.'

'*They* can't? Why do you talk to me about them? I'm not engaged to them.'

'Oh, Francie, *I* am! And it's they who are buried beneath that filthy rubbish!'

She flushed at this characterisation of Mr Flack's epistle; then she said in a softer voice: 'I'm very sorry—very sorry indeed. But evidently I'm not delicate.'

He looked at her, helpless and bitter. 'It's not the newspapers, in your country, that would have made you so. Lord, they're too incredible! And the ladies have them on their tables.'

'You told me we couldn't here—that the Paris ones are too bad,' said Francie.

'Bad they are, God knows; but they have never published anything like that—poured forth such a flood of impudence on decent, quiet people who only want to be left alone.'

Francie sank into a chair by the table, as if she were too tired to stand longer, and with her arms spread out on the lamp-lit plush she looked up at him. 'Was it there you saw it?'

'Yes, a few days before I sailed. I hated them from the moment I got there—I looked at them very little. But that was a chance. I opened the paper in the hall of an hotel (there was a big marble floor and spittoons!) and my eyes fell upon that horror. It made me ill.'

'Did you think it was me?'

'About as soon as I supposed it was my father. But I was too mystified, too tormented.'

'Then why didn't you write to me, if you didn't think it was me?'

'Write to you? I wrote to you every three days.'

'Not after that.'

'Well, I may have omitted a post at the last—I thought it might be Delia,' Gaston added in a moment.

'Oh, she didn't want me to do it—the day I went with him, the day I told him. She tried to prevent me.'

'Would to God then she had!'

'Haven't you told them she's delicate too?' Francie asked, in her strange tone.

Gaston made no answer to this; but he broke out—'What power, in heaven's name, has he got over you? What spell has he worked?'

'He's an old friend—he helped us ever so much when we were first in Paris.'

'But, my dearest child, what friends—what a man to know!'

'If we hadn't known him we shouldn't have known you. Remember that it was Mr Flack who brought us that day to Mr Waterlow's.'

'Oh, you would have come some other way,' said Gaston.

'Not in the least. We knew nothing about any other way. He helped us in everything—he showed us everything. That was why I told him—when he asked me. I liked him for what he had done.'

Gaston, who had now also seated himself, listened to this attentively. 'I see. It was a kind of delicacy.'

'Oh, a kind!' She smiled.

He remained a little with his eyes on her face. 'Was it for me?'

'Of course it was for you.'

'Ah, how strange you are!' he exclaimed, tenderly. 'Such contradictions—*on s'y perd*. I wish you would say that to *them*, that way. Everything would be right.'

'Never, never!' said the girl. 'I have wronged them, and nothing will ever be the same again. It was fatal. If I felt as they do I too would loathe the person who should have done such a thing. It doesn't seem to me so bad—the thing in the paper; but you know best. You must go back to them. You know best,' she repeated.

'They were the last, the last people in France, to do it to. The sense of excruciation—of pollution,' Gaston rejoined, making his reflections audibly.

'Oh, you needn't tell me—I saw them all there!' Francie exclaimed.

'It must have been a dreadful scene. But you *didn't* brave them, did you?'

'Brave them—what are you talking about? To you that idea is incredible!'

'No, it isn't,' he said, gently.

'Well, go back to them—go back,' she repeated. At this he half threw himself across the table, to seize her hands; but she drew away and, as he came nearer, pushed her chair back, springing up. 'You know you didn't come here to tell me you are ready to give them up.'

He rose to his feet, slowly. 'To give them up? I have

been battling with them till I'm ready to drop. You don't know how they feel—how they *must* feel.'

'Oh yes, I do. All this has made me older, every hour.'

'It has made you more beautiful,' said Gaston Probert.

'I don't care. Nothing will induce me to consent to any sacrifice.'

'Some sacrifice there must be. Give me time—give me time, I'll manage it. I only wish they hadn't seen you there in the Bois.'

'In the Bois?'

'That Marguerite hadn't seen you—with that blackguard. That's the image they can't get over.'

'I see you can't either, Gaston. Well, I *was* there and I was very happy. That's all I can say. You must take me as I am.'

'Don't—don't; you infuriate me!' he pleaded, frowning.

Francie had seemed to soften, but she was in a sudden flame again. 'Of course I do, and I shall do it again. We are too different. Everything makes you so. You can't give them up —ever, ever. Good-bye—good-bye! That's all I wanted to tell you.'

'I'll go and throttle him!' Gaston said, lugubriously.

'Very well, go! Good-bye.' She had stepped quickly to the door and had already opened it, vanishing as she had done the last time.

'Francie, Francie!' he exclaimed, following her into the passage. The door was not the one that led into the salon; it communicated with the other apartments. The girl had plunged into these—he already heard her locking herself in. Presently he went away, without taking leave of Mr Dosson and Delia.

'Why, he acts just like Mr Flack,' said the old man, when they discovered that the interview in the dining-room had come to an end.

The next day was a bad day for Charles Waterlow. His work, in the Avenue de Villiers, was terribly interrupted. Gaston Probert invited himself to breakfast with him at noon and remained till the time at which the artist usually went out—an extravagance partly justified by a previous separation of several weeks. During these three or four hours Gaston walked up and down the studio, while Waterlow either sat or stood before his easel. He put his host out vastly and acted on his nerves, but Waterlow was patient with him because he was very sorry for him, feeling the occasion to be a great crisis. His compassion, it is true, was slightly tinged with contempt: nevertheless he looked at the case generously, perceived it to be one in which a friend should be a friend—in which he, in particular, might see the distracted fellow through. Gaston was in a fever; he broke out into passionate arguments which were succeeded by fits of gloomy silence. He roamed about continually, with his hands in his pockets and his hair in a tangle; he could take neither a decision nor a momentary rest. It struck Waterlow more than ever before that he was after all essentially a foreigner; he had the sensibility of one, the sentimental candour, the need for sympathy, the communicative despair. A real young Anglo-Saxon would have buttoned himself up in his embarrassment and been dry and awkward and capable and unconscious of a drama; but Gaston was effusive and appealing and ridiculous and graceful— natural, above all, and egotistical. Indeed, a real young Anglo-Saxon would not have had this particular embarrassment at all for he would not have parted to such an extent with his moral independence. It was this weakness that excited Waterlow's secret scorn: family feeling was all very well, but to see it erected into a superstition affected him very much in the same way as the image of a blackamoor upon his knees before a fetish. He now measured for the first time the root it had taken in Gaston's nature. To act like a man the poor fellow must pull up the root, but the operation was terribly painful— was attended with cries and tears and contortions, with baffling scruples and a sense of sacrilege, the sense of siding with strangers against his own flesh and blood. Every now and then he broke out—'And if you see her— as she looks just now (she's too lovely—too touching!) you would see how right I was originally—when I found in her such a revelation of that type, the French Renaissance, you know, the one we talked about.' But he reverted with at least equal frequency to the idea that he seemed unable to throw off, that it was like something done on purpose, with a refinement of cruelty; such an accident to *them*, of all people on earth, the very last, the very last, those who he verily believed would feel it more than any family in the world. When Waterlow asked what made them so exceptionally ticklish he could only say that they just happened to be so; it was his father's influence, his very genius, the worship of privacy and good manners, a hatred of all the new familiarities and profanations. The artist inquired further, at last, rather wearily, what in two words was the practical question his friend desired that he should consider. Whether he should be justified in throwing over Miss Francina—was that it?

'Oh heavens, no! For what sneak do you take me? She made a mistake, but any one might do that. It's whether it strikes you that I should be justified in throwing *them* over.'

'It depends upon the sense you attach to justification.'

'I mean—should I be miserably unhappy—would it be in their power to make me so?'

'To try—certainly, if they are capable of anything so nasty. The only honourable conduct for them is to let you alone.'

'Ah, they won't do that—they like me too much,' Gaston said, ingenuously.

'It's an odd way of liking. The best way to show that would be to let you marry the girl you love.'

'Certainly—but they are profoundly convinced that she represents such dangers, such vulgarities, such possibilities of doing other things of the same sort, that it's upon *them* my happiness would be shattered.'

'Well, if you yourself have no secret for persuading them of the contrary I'm afraid I can't teach you one.'

'Yes, I ought to do it myself,' said Gaston, in the candour of his meditations. Then he went on, in his torment of inconsistency—'They never believed in her from the first. My father was perfectly definite about it. At heart they never accepted her; they only pretended to do so because I guaranteed that she was incapable of doing a thing that could ever displease them. Then no sooner was my back turned than she perpetrated that!'

'That was your folly,' Waterlow remarked, painting away.

'My folly—to turn my back?'

'No, no—to guarantee.'

'My dear fellow—wouldn't you?' Gaston asked, staring.

'Never in the world.'

'You would have thought her capable——?'

'*Capabilissima!* and I shouldn't have cared.'

'Do you think her then capable of doing it again?'

'I don't care if she is; that's the least of all questions.'

'The least?'

'Ah, don't you see, wretched youth,' said Waterlow, pausing from his work and looking up—'don't you see that the question of her possibilities is as nothing compared to that of yours? She's the sweetest young thing I ever saw; but even if she happened not to be I should urge you to marry her, in simple self-preservation.'

'In self-preservation?'

'To rescue from destruction the last remnant of your independence. That's a much more important matter even

than not treating her shabbily. They are doing their best
to kill you morally—to render you incapable of individual life.'

'They are—they are!' Gaston declared, with enthusiasm.

'Well then, if you believe it, for heaven's sake go and
marry her to-morrow!' Waterlow threw down his imple-
ments and added, 'And come out of this—into the air.'

Gaston, however, was planted in his path on the way
to the door. 'And if she does break out again, in the same
way?'

'In the same way?'

'In some other manifestation of that terrible order?'

'Well,' said Waterlow, 'you will at least have got rid
of your family.'

'Yes, if she does that I shall be glad they are not there!
They're right, *pourtant*, they're right,' Gaston went on,
passing out of the studio with his friend.

'They're right?'

'It was a dreadful thing.'

'Yes, thank heaven! It was the finger of providence, to
give you your chance.' This was ingenious, but, though
he could glow for a moment in response to it, Francie's
lover—if lover he may in his most infirm aspect be called
—looked as if he mistrusted it, thought it slightly sophis-
tical. What really shook him however was his companion's saying to him in the vestibule, when they had
taken their hats and sticks and were on the point of going
out: 'Lord, man, how can you be so impenetrably dense?

Don't you see that she's really of the softest, finest material that breathes, that she's a perfect flower of plasticity, that everything you may have an apprehension about will drop away from her like the dead leaves from a rose and that you may make of her any perfect and enchanting thing you yourself have the wit to conceive?'

'Ah, my dear friend!' Gaston Probert murmured, gratefully, panting.

'The limit will be yours, not hers,' Waterlow added.

'No, no, I have done with limits,' his companion rejoined, ecstatically.

That evening at ten o'clock Gaston went to the Hôtel de l'Univers et de Cheltenham and requested the German waiter to introduce him into the dining-room attached to Mr Dosson's apartments and then go and tell Miss Francina he was awaiting her there.

'Oh, you'll be better there than in the zalon—they have villed it with the luccatch,' said the man, who always addressed him in an intention of English and was not ignorant of the tie that united the visitor to the amiable American family, or perhaps even of the modifications it had lately undergone.

'With their luggage?'

'They leave to-morrow morning—oh, I don't think they themselves know for where, sir.'

'Please then say to Miss Francina that I have called on very urgent business—that I'm pressed, pressed!'

The eagerness of the sentiment which possessed Gaston at that moment is communicative, but perhaps the vividness with which the waiter placed it before the young lady is better explained by the fact that her lover slipped a five-franc piece into his hand. At any rate she entered the dining-room sooner than Gaston had ventured to hope, though she corrected this promptitude a little by stopping short, drawing back, when she saw how pale he was and how she looked as if he had been crying.

'I have chosen—I have chosen,' he said gently, smiling at her in contradiction to these indications.

'You have chosen?'

'I have had to give them up. But I like it so much better than having to give *you* up! I took you first with their assent. That was well enough—it was worth trying for. But now I take you without it. We can live that way too.'

'Ah, I'm not worth it. You give up too much!' cried the girl. 'We're going away—it's all over.' She turned from him quickly, as if to carry out her meaning, but he caught her more quickly still and held her—held her fast and long. She had only freed herself when her father and sister broke in, from the salon, attracted apparently by the audible commotion.

'Oh, I thought you had at least knocked over the lamp!' Delia exclaimed.

'You must take me with you if you are going away, Mr Dosson,' Gaston said. 'I will start whenever you like.'

'All right—where shall we go?' the old man asked.

'Hadn't you decided that?'

'Well, the girls said they would tell me.'

'We were going home,' said Francie.

'No we weren't—not a bit!' Delia declared.

'Oh, not there,' Gaston murmured, pathetically, looking at Francie.

'Well, when you've fixed it you can take the tickets,' Mr Dosson observed.

'To some place where there are no newspapers,' Gaston went on.

'I guess you'll have hard work to find one.'

'Dear me, we needn't read them! We wouldn't have read that one if your family hadn't forced us,' Delia said to her prospective brother-in-law.

'Well, I shall never be forced—I shall never again in my life look at one,' he replied.

'You'll see—you'll have to!' laughed Mr Dosson.

'No, you'll tell us enough.'

Francie had her eyes on the ground; they were all smiling but she. 'Won't they forgive me, ever?' she asked, looking up.

'Yes, perfectly, if you can persuade me not to marry you. But in that case what good will their forgiveness do you?'

'Well, perhaps it's better to pay for it.'

'To pay for it?'

'By suffering something. For it *was* dreadful.'

'Oh, for all you'll suffer——!' Gaston exclaimed, shining down at her.

'It was for you—only for you, as I told you,' the girl went on.

'Yes, don't tell me again—I don't like that explanation! I ought to let you know that my father now declines to do anything for me,' the young man added, to Mr Dosson.

'To do anything for you?'

'To give me any money.'

'Well, that makes me feel better,' said Mr Dosson.

'There'll be enough for all—especially if we economise in newspapers,' Delia declared, jocosely.

'Well, I don't know, after all—the *Reverberator* came for nothing,' her father went on, in the same spirit.

'Don't you be afraid he'll ever send it now!' cried the girl.

'I'm very sorry—because they were lovely,' Francie said to Gaston, with sad eyes.

'Let us wait to say that till they come back to us,' Gaston returned, somewhat sententiously. He really cared little at this moment whether his relatives were lovely or not.

'I'm sure you won't have to wait long!' Delia remarked, with the same cheerfulness.

' "Till they come back"?' Mr Dosson repeated. 'Ah, they can't come back now. We won't take them in!' The words fell from his lips with a mild unexpected austerity which imposed itself, producing a momentary silence, and it is a sign of Gaston's complete emancipation that he did not in his heart resent this image of eventual favours denied to his race. The resentment was rather Delia's, but she kept it to herself, for she was capable of reflecting with complacency that the key of the house would after all be hers, so that she could open the door for the Proberts if they should knock. Now that her sister's marriage was really to take place her consciousness that the American people would have been told so was still more agreeable. The party left the Hôtel de l'Univers et de Cheltenham on the morrow, but it appeared to the German waiter, as he accepted another five-franc piece from the happy and now reckless Gaston, that they were even yet not at all clear as to where they were going.

THE END

OTHER GROVE PRESS DRAMA
AND THEATER PAPERBACKS

GROVE PRESS, INC., 196 West Houston St., New York, N.Y. 10014